TALES *of the* MOCHI WALA

The Cobbler

AF516787

A Journey Through Mystic Indian Folklore

TALES

of the

MOCHI WALA

The Cobbler

"Timeless stories remind us that imagination belongs to everyone, both the young and the wise."

S.K. Luke

Copyright

Tales of the Mochi Wala - The Cobbler

S.K. Luke

First Edition, 2025
© S.K. Luke, 2025. All rights reserved.
No part of this publication may be reproduced, stored in a retrieval system, or transmitted in any form or by any means—electronic, mechanical, photo-copying, recording, or otherwise—without the author's or publisher's prior written permission.
This is a work of fiction. Names, characters, places, incidents, and dialogues are products of the author's imagination or used fictitiously. Any resemblance to actual persons, living or deceased, events or locations is entirely coincidental.

Requests for permission or inquiries should be directed to the author.

ISBN: 978-93-342-5093-0

Dedication

To all those who cherish their childhood memories, Where innocence thrived and laughter knew no bounds.

Childhood friends are not just friends; they are companions for life

Also, by ***S. K. Luke,***
Available as both eBook and Paperback editions on Amazon Global and IngramSpark, making it accessible to readers worldwide.

Fictional

Milo the Cat – A Day Out

Villy the Vulture

Jeron and John – High and Fly

Ben the Bear

Who's in the ATTIC

Adventures of Binny n Bonny

Bella's Boat Escapade

Silence Whispers

Non-Fictional

Decoding Maturity

Navigating The Grey

Contents

Prologue

Rekindled Journey

In our childhood, life was simple, untouched by gadgets or endless distractions. We had each other, boundless curiosity, and the magic of stories that shaped our world. At the heart of it all was the Mochi Wala.

He wasn't just a cobbler but a storyteller, a weaver of dreams. His tiny shop, nestled in the village's corner, was a portal to mystical lands. Tales of a magical wallet that could conceal treasures, a clever cobbler who outwitted bandits, mischievous Yakshas stealing a priest's sandals, a tone-deaf singer charming spirits with his off-key notes, or a fisherman battling a cunning Rakshasa came alive as we sat on his creaky bench or the dusty ground, captivated by his voice. Amid the scent of leather and the rhythmic tapping of tools, he transported us to extraordinary worlds.

Each story carried hidden lessons—kindness, courage, resilience, and the beauty of dreams. The Mochi Wala didn't just entertain us; he opened our eyes to the magic in everyday life, teaching us to find the extraordinary in the ordinary.

But time marched on, pulling us away from his shop and those cherished tales. As we grew up, his stories faded into distant echoes, buried beneath the responsibilities of adulthood. Yet, when we reunited years later, his name was the first to come up. Over laughter and nostalgia, we recounted his tales, feeling a bittersweet longing to reconnect with him.

Where was he now? Had the years changed him, or was he still spinning stories for young hearts? This thought consumed us, driving us on a journey—not just to meet the man who shaped our childhood but to reclaim a part of ourselves.

When we finally found him, he had aged—his hair greyer, his hands slower—but his spirit remained unchanged. His twinkling eyes, warm smile, and magical voice returned us to those carefree afternoons. While he projected happiness to all, he had endured a hidden turmoil of love and sacrifice. Uncovering this, we were privileged to reunite him with his lost love, rekindling a part of his life he thought was gone.

As he welcomed us, it felt as though no time had passed. We were children again, wide-eyed and eager, ready to be whisked away into his enchanting worlds. The Mochi Wala taught us a truth we hadn't fully grasped before: magic isn't something you find—it's something you create. His stories weren't just entertainment; they were a gift, a lens to see wonder in the world.

Now, when life feels overwhelming, I think of him. His tales remind me to pause, dream, and embrace the small joys. The Mochi Wala wasn't just a storyteller—he was our guide, showing us how to turn the ordinary into the extraordinary.

Welcome to A Journey Through Mystic Indian Folk Tales. These stories pay tribute to Mochi Wala's magic in our lives. May they inspire you to find the same enchantment that surrounds you, waiting to be discovered.

Down the Memory Lane

It all began with a reunion plan, a chance to rekindle old friendships and create new memories. We seldom kept in touch with each other; our busy lives and commitments got the better of us. Despite our busy lives and commitments, we stayed connected on and off through group chats, albeit sporadically.

As we got caught up - with each other's lives, we realised that our busyness had been an excuse for neglecting what truly matters. We vowed to prioritise our relationships, make time for meaningful connections, and appreciate the simple moments in life. Our online interactions were often limited to forwarded messages, jokes, and birthday wishes. The conversations were superficial, lacking the depth and warmth of our past connections.

Our online conversations had become shallow and mechanical. Gone were the days of lively discussions and meaningful connections. We'd resorted to lazy communication, relying on forwarded messages and jokes to fill the void. Even those attempts at humour often fell flat, met with silence or a mere handful of reactions. It was as if we'd lost the art of conversation and content to exist in the same digital space without engaging.

The only exception was birthdays when our group chat would come alive with well-wishes and pleasantries. But even those exchanges felt shallow.

"Hey, I thought your birthday was next month."

"You don't look old for your age."

"Age is just a number."

"Where are we meeting for a party?"

These hollow exchanges left me wondering: had we become so accustomed to the ease of digital communication that we'd forgotten the value of genuine connection? Were we going through the motions, or could we rekindle the spark that once brought us together?

We've become so ensnared in our worlds that we've forgotten to cherish the small, free pleasures that bring us joy. We've adopted a mindset where "free" is synonymous with "worthless," and we're willing to pay a premium for happiness. When did I last feel the soft grass beneath my bare feet? I can't recall. We're so caught up in our pursuits that we neglect the simple things. We invest in luxurious homes but rarely utilise the amenities we pay for. We find happiness in seeing our children enjoy them but sometimes neglect our pleasure.

We're running in the wrong direction, chasing expensive thrills while disregarding the free delights surrounding us. We need to rebalance and rediscover the beauty in everyday moments. Let's step back, remove our shoes, and feel the grass beneath our feet. Let's relearn to appreciate the small, free joys that bring us contentment and smiles.

Reunion Trails - "On the day of our reunion, I was the first to arrive. I checked the invite calendar to be sure I had the date correct. I was just early, that's all. It was a relief to know that we were meeting today, and I hoped there would be no hiccups or last-minute cancellations."

I stood in the village where we spent most of our childhood. But as I looked around, I was struck by how much had changed. The town was no longer the quaint, peaceful place I remembered. It had transformed into a bustling hub with concrete structures, wider roads, and a surge of new faces.

I felt like a stranger in a place that was once my home. The familiarity was gone, replaced by an eerie sense of disconnection. I decided to explore, hoping to find some remnants of the past. Walking through a narrow lane leading to my old rented house, I was met with nostalgia and disorientation.

The lane was unchanged, but the faces were new. I scanned the surroundings, searching for a glimpse of recognition, but it seemed like everyone I knew had vanished, replaced by strangers. The houses, though unchanged, seemed to hold secrets and stories that no longer belonged to me.

I continued walking, lost in thought, trying to reconcile the past with the present. The village, once a testament to our carefree childhood, now seemed like a distant memory, fading away with each passing moment.

Familiar Acquaintance - As I approached my childhood home, a faint voice called out to me, filled with warmth and familiarity. I turned to see an old lady seated outside her doorstep, her face lit up with a bright smile. She beckoned me over, her hands waving in excitement. Her husband emerged from the house, and she whispered something to him. His eyes sparkled with recognition, and he exclaimed, "You're all grown up! How's your mum?"

The old couple's faces were etched with memories of my family, particularly my mother, who was an integral part of the village community. They fondly recalled my younger brother's mischievous ways, especially his penchant for throwing water at passersby.

The old lady's eyes twinkled with mirth as she asked, "How is he now? Does he still play pranks on people?"

Their genuine interest in my family's well-being touched my heart. I smiled, feeling a deep connection to this place and its people.

"Mum is doing fine," I replied. "My siblings are all grown up now, but I'm sure my brother still has a spark of mischief."

The old couple chuckled, and we exchanged more stories, bridging the gap of years. At that moment, I felt like I had come home, surrounded by people who knew me and my family's history.

As I smiled and responded to their questions, I couldn't help but wonder who these familiar strangers were. And then, like a sudden burst of memory, it hit me. The old lady was once my teacher, and her appeal and kindness are still in my mind. The older man, her husband, was the taxi driver who often took us on adventures around the village.

I felt a shiver run down my spine as I recalled their youthful energy and vitality. They were once the newlywed couple who had moved in next door, and my mother had helped them settle into their new home. I remembered being sent to deliver a food tiffin to their house, a small act of kindness that had sparked a connection.

Time had weathered their faces, but their eyes still sparkled with warmth and recognition. I felt a deep sense of nostalgia wash over me as my childhood memories came flooding back. The old lady's warmness, the older man's stories of adventure, and my mother's kindness swirled together in a bittersweet mix of past and present.

I shared the updates of my family's life, my voice filled with pride and warmth. "My brother is all grown up, married, and has two kids of his own now," I said, a smile spreading across my face.

The old couple's eyes lit up with delight, their faces reflecting their genuine interest. I continued, "My mum and dad are also doing well. My dad is retired and enjoying his retired life, surrounded by love and comfort."

I paused, collecting my thoughts before adding, "My younger sister is married and has two grown-up kids. All are doing well, and we're grateful for the blessings in our lives."

The old couple nodded, their faces beaming with happiness. They exchanged a warm glance, and I could sense their joy in seeing the next generation thrive. We sat there momentarily, basking in the warmth of shared memories and the comfort of knowing that life had been kind to us.

I asked about their well-being and was genuinely interested in their lives. The older woman's face lit up with a warm smile. "I've retired from teaching, and our kids are grown up and married. We're proud grandparents now."

The old man added, "We prefer our independence, living independently, but we visit our kids when we can. I still drive my cab; it keeps me active and engaged." Their tone hinted at a subtle sadness, a story untold, but they bravely kept it hidden.

Their eyes sparkled with hospitality as they invited me in for chai. I declined graciously, explaining my upcoming reunion with friends. They understood, and we exchanged warm farewells. As I turned to leave, I sensed a deep appreciation for this chance encounter. We reconnected, sharing moments from our past and present. Though time had weathered their faces, their kindness and warmth remained unchanged.

Home Sweet Home - "Home is where your family resides, but the homes you leave behind are memories galore." - As I passed by the house where I spent my childhood, a wave of longing washed over me. The once-familiar single-story dwelling with a red-tiled roof had transformed into a three-story apartment complex home to multiple families. The landlord's son had taken over, but that's a story for another time.

I paused, memories flooding my mind. Our one-room rented house, where the kitchen, hall, and bedroom merged into one, seemed like a distant dream. The outdoor toilets, shared among tenants, brought back memories of waiting in line, sometimes for ages, and the occasional rush to the nearby fields to answer nature's call.

But now, those fields were replaced by a concrete jungle of houses and people. I felt a pang of sadness, witnessing the drastic change. Our childhood's simplicity and the freedom to roam and play seemed lost forever. Yet, amidst the concrete chaos, my heart held onto the memories of a carefree childhood, a reminder of the joy and laughter that once filled those streets.

Leaving that home was bittersweet. It was hard to say goodbye to the place where I had so many firsts—first steps, first words, first friends. But the memories we made there are etched in my heart forever. I am filled with warmth and nostalgia whenever I think of that house.

I recall those carefree days, playing in lush green meadows and lawns, exploring sugarcane farms, and savouring green mangoes. The thrill of evading farmers, who chased us with sticks and stones, still brings a smile. One incident stands out—when a stone hit my friend's foot, he ran in fear, not stopping until he felt safe. I remember rushing home to fetch turmeric powder to treat his wound, our makeshift remedy.

Years later, we reunited at his father's funeral and ruminated about old times. The memory of that stone-pelting incident resurfaced, and we exchanged gentle grins. My friend's words still echo: "I'll never forget those good old days; it was worth the memories we shared." Though he returned to the US and won't join our reunion today, his spirit will be with us.

Selfless heroism - As I reminisce about my childhood, I am reminded of a remarkable incident in this vicinity. It's a story that highlights the selflessness and kindness of strangers, which is a rarity in today's world.

My younger brother was fascinated by television, but we couldn't afford one at home. So, he often visited our neighbours' houses to watch TV programs. They would welcome him with open arms and even offer him food if he stayed on to watch his favourite shows during odd hours. However, my father thought it was time we had our TV, and he managed to purchase a black and white one he could afford.

The TV arrived on a Sunday, and we were excited to watch our first program together. But as we sat in front of the TV, my father asked, "Where's your younger brother?" We realised he was missing, and just then, a stranger appeared at our doorstep, followed by our neighbours. He was drenched in water, wet hair and clothes, and carried my brother in his arms. My brother was also damp and looked like he had been through a traumatic experience.

The stranger, a mason, explained that he had been working nearby when he saw my brother fall into the well. Without hesitation, he jumped into the well, which was about fifty meters away, and saved my brother from drowning. He described the water as greenish and murky, making it difficult to spot my brother. Despite the challenges, he managed to rescue and bring him to safety.

What struck us most was the stranger's selflessness. He had risked his own life to save my brother without caring about the documents, money, or notes he had in his pocket, which were all soaked in water.

When my father offered him money as a token of gratitude, the stranger declined and said, "I'm just a mason, and I did what any human would do in that situation." He didn't leave his name or wait for our thanks before returning to work.

This incident has left an indelible mark on our lives. The stranger's actions were a testament to the kindness and compassion that exists in humanity. He gave my brother a second chance at life, saved our family from immense grief, and demonstrated that true heroism is about selfless acts without expectation of reward or recognition.

Friendly Vibes - As I stood there, taking in the sights and sounds of my childhood haunts, I felt a deep sense of melancholy wash over me.

The familiar names – "Madhu Stationaries" and "Ganesh Cycle Mart" - transported me back to a time when life was simpler, and friendships were forged over shared adventures.

Madhu's father, now grey-haired and frail, still operated the shop with his son. Their warm smiles and gentle nods acknowledged our shared past, even as they tended to their customers. I couldn't linger long, but the brief encounter left an indelible mark on my heart.

Across the narrow road, Ganesh's cycle shop bustled with activity. His absence was puzzling, but the counter attendant's inquiry about my name sparked a chain reaction. Ganesh emerged from the adjacent room, his eyes locking onto mine with a hint of recognition. Time had transformed his physique, but the mischievous glint in his eye remained unchanged.

The years melted away instantly, and we were once again the carefree children who roamed these streets, exploring every nook and cranny. The reunion was a poignant reminder that some bonds transcend time and distance, waiting to be rekindled when the moment is right.

Age is a mere number to some, yet a profound force that reshapes our lives. As our bodies grow older, our appearance and experiences mould our outlook. Though our hearts may remain young, our physical transformation prompts introspection.

Life's fleeting nature becomes apparent, and we ponder the passage of time. In our youth, ambition drives us to chase dreams, meet requirements, and fulfil commitments.

We often overlook the small, seemingly insignificant moments. However, as time takes its toll, these minuscule memories become precious. We attempt to relive our lives through them, cherishing the beauty of nostalgia.

Our priorities shift, and we begin to appreciate the tiny details we once disregarded. Memories, once trivial, now hold immense value. We realise that life's essence lies not in grand achievements but in the subtle, everyday experiences that make us human.

I got deviated for a moment. So where were we?

Aha. Yes!!

As Ganesh and I reunited, our conversation flowed effortlessly, like no time had passed. We delved into the treasure trove of memories, reliving moments that defined our childhood. One such incident, long buried, resurfaced, bringing laughter and wistfulness.

The memory of our bicycle escapade still evokes a smile. We were around 5-7 years old, and our desire for adventure led us to rent a bicycle for ten paisa an hour.

Ganesh's father, the cycle shop owner, would often lend us a bike, unaware of the thrills we sought. We chose a small bicycle on this particular day, perfect for our age and size.

With Ganesh perched on the carrier and me on the main seat, we began our ascent up the hill. We planned to ride down together, feeling the wind in our hair and the adrenaline rush in our veins.

However, our youthful enthusiasm clouded our judgment, and we misjudged the slope's steepness. As we rolled down the hill, our screams of excitement turned to cries for help.

The bicycle suffered damage, but we escaped with only bruises. A familiar face appeared as we struggled to lift the bike - the cobbler who often regaled us with stories and jokes.

He helped us transport the bike back to Ganesh's father, who was furious but eventually softened upon seeing our injuries.

The memory of that day remains etched in my mind, a testament to childhood's unbridled joy and mischief. Sharing this story with my mum would undoubtedly bring a smile to her face and a hint of surprise at our daring adventure.

As we reminisced about old times, I asked Ganesh about the cobbler who had helped us on that fateful day. "What happened to him?" I inquired, curiosity getting the better of me.

Ganesh's expression turned sombre, and he replied, "I remember it like it was yesterday. I was in my teens when we heard that the cobbler had vanished. No one saw him again, and his disappearance remained a mystery."

"He continued, 'The landlord had to break open the cobbler's shop and remove all his belongings. The shop was then rented to someone else. After that, it changed hands, and we saw new tenants over a couple of years. We never knew what happened to the Mochi Wala.'" The plot - The cobbler's mysterious disappearance left an air of intrigue, a reminder that some secrets remain unsolved and some stories untold.

The memory of his kindness and help during our childhood adventure would stay with us, even as the circumstances of his vanishing remained a puzzle. As I chatted with Ganesh, my phone rang, breaking the spell of nostalgia.

My friends were waiting for me at the meeting point, and I knew I had to leave. I quickly ended my reunion with Ganesh, exchanging contact numbers and promising to stay in touch. With a mix of sadness and joy, I bid farewell to my old friend and our shared memories.

I left the shop, carrying the warmth of our reunion and the promise of rekindled friendship. As I walked towards the meeting point, I couldn't help but feel grateful for the unexpected encounter. The chance meeting had brought back a flood of memories, reminding me of the joy and simplicity of childhood friendships.

A Joyful Reunion

As I strolled through the familiar streets, I turned and looked back at the old Mochi Wala shop, transporting me back in time. Memories came flooding back, and I couldn't help but pause, gazing at the unchanged facade. While surrounding shops had transformed, this humble abode remained frozen in time.

Curiosity got the better of me, and I pondered the reasons behind its steadfast appearance. Was it the landlord's financial constraints or a deliberate choice to preserve its sentimental charm? The questions swirled in my mind as I continued my walk.

A Nostalgic Encounter - The serendipity of the moment was not lost on me, for soon, I found myself face to face with old friends, their familiar smiles a testament to the enduring bonds of time. The unexpected encounter was a poignant reminder that some things, like true friendships and wistful memories, remain unchanged, even as the world around us evolves.

Our eyes locked on one another, the years melted away, and they were transported back to a time when life was simpler. The warmth of their smiles and the excitement in their voices was palpable as they rushed towards each other, arms open wide.

The air was filled with laughter and chatter as they enveloped each other in tight hugs, holding on for a moment longer than necessary. It was as if they were trying to make up for lost time, to recapture the bond they once shared.

As they pulled back to gaze at each other, their eyes sparkled with happiness, and their faces glowed with a sense of belonging; they stood there laughing and grinning, happier than life itself to see each other after ages; once roamed carefree, with black, uncombed, wavy hair dancing in the wind, flat tummies and lean frames, full of energy and life, torn shoes and slippers, a testament to their adventurous spirits, ragged clothing, worn with pride and a sense of freedom.

But time, the significant modifier, has woven its magic with a fast-forward button, watching them now with white hair crowning their wise and weathered heads, bold patches of grey, a distinguished mark of their journeys, tummies that resemble watermelon fields, a sign of life's indulgences, polished and swagged-up looks, a far cry from their rugged past, their hands, once clutching marble stones, used in fierce competitions, wooden sticks, wielded like mighty swords, kites, soaring high in the sky, symbols of their dreams.

Now, holding cell phones in their hands as if in separable, current gateways to a world of information and connection, time may have changed their appearance. Still, the spark in their eyes remains, a testament to the enduring spirit of youth.

We stepped into a small restaurant; lush sugarcane fields once surrounded its walls. Now a distant memory, the village had given way to modern civilisation's relentless march.

Yet, amidst the change, our gathering remained a constant, a testament to the enduring power of friendship

As we settled into a cosy corner table, some sat while others stood, engaged in lively chatter. Eventually, we all sat down, ordering chai without sugar – a nod to the health concerns that came with age.

As we sipped our chai, the cares of our lives – the pains, sorrows, and shortcomings – faded into the background.

We were lost in the joy of each other's company, reminiscing and laughing together.

At that moment, we knew that friends are the best medicine, priceless and irreplaceable. The reunion celebrated their enduring friendship, a testament to the power of connections that last a lifetime.

A Lingering Enigma - As I revealed in the warmth of reunion with my friends, a lingering thought persisted, like a gentle hum in the background.

The cobbler, once a familiar figure, had vanished Without a trace. His sudden disappearance remained a mystery, leaving behind only unanswered questions.

No one knew his whereabouts, and the fact that he never returned to claim his belongings from the shop deepened the enigma.

It was as if he had vanished into thin air, leaving behind a void that seemed impossible to fill.

Even amidst the joy of reconnecting with old friends, my mind wandered back to the cobbler, wondering what had become of him and whether he was at peace. The memory of his gentle smile and skilled hands, once so full of life, now seemed like a fleeting dream.

Without warning, I blurted out, “Do you remember the Mochi Wala?” and the room fell silent. Eyes darted around, searching for answers, but none came. The sudden pause was palpable, with some puzzled by the query and others eager to see where it would lead. Then, like a dam breaking, memories burst forth.

One friend’s voice filled the void, “I remember those rainy days when we’d seek refuge in the cobbler’s shop. We’d watch, mesmerised, as he worked his magic on leather shoes and slippers. And in his spare moments, he’d spin tales that transported us to another world.”

The conversation took a life of its own as each friend chimed in with their own Mochi Wala encounter. Laughter and nods of recognition filled the air as the memories flowed like a river. The question unlocked a treasure trove of shared experiences, binding them together in a way only nostalgia can.

“I still remember the story he told us about...” my friend’s voice trailed off, lost in thought. The place leaned in, anticipation hanging in the air like a challenge.

“The priest who did not buy sandals!” another friend exclaimed, eyes lighting up with excitement.

"Or was it the tale of the singer who was ridiculed with sandals because of his obnoxious singing!" my friend exclaimed, correcting the others with a chuckle.

We burst into laughter, the story's absurdity sparking a chain reaction of giggles and snorts. "Oh yes! I remember now!" someone said, "He used to sing off-key, and people would throw sandals at him to shut him up!"

Once forgotten, Mochi Wala's tale comes flooding back, its ridiculousness and humour transporting us back to a time when laughter was pure and unadulterated. The memory of the singer's obnoxious tunes and the sandals that rained upon him symbolises the joy and camaraderie we shared in those simple, carefree days.

The debate sparked a flurry of memories, each friend recalling a different story yet sharing a common thread – the Mochi Wala's mesmerising tales. The place erupted in a chorus of laughter and nods as the friends relived the magic of those moments.

In that instant, Mochi Wala's legacy came alive, his stories woven into the fabric of their shared history, a testament to the power of memory and friendship.

The noise we were generating was quite disturbing for other customers seated in the restaurant. The manager approached us and politely asked us to keep our voices low.

The joy of meeting old friends made us behave like children, having no contentment in ourselves, filled with joy and laughter, and simply giggling away.

A detour -With a collective desire to break free from the confines of the restaurant, we -decided to head to the riverside, a suggestion that met with unanimous approval. After settling the bill, we poured out of the restaurant, eager to embark on our next adventure.

Travelling in two cars, we opted for a cosy, lap-sitting arrangement, redolent of our carefree childhood days. As we drove towards the river, the village night market came into view, its vibrant stalls and vendors evoking memories of my childhood excursions with my mum.

We would visit this market daily, selecting the freshest produce, fruits, and dairy products. The market's name, "night market," seemed incongruous, as it operated from sunrise to sunset. Yet, the moniker stuck, a testament to the market's enduring charm.

As we passed, the market's familiarity was comforting, a reminder that some things remain constant amidst the passage of time. Our riverside escapade awaited, promising a night of unbridled joy and camaraderie.

Riverside Revelry—As we arrived at the riverside, we discovered a secluded spot to park our cars surrounded by wilderness. We disembarked, eager to immerse ourselves in nature's serenity. A short walk led us to the river's edge, where we

We found various rocks perfect for sitting and dipping our legs in the cool water.Some of us preferred to keep our feet dry, hurl stones or dip twigs into the river's gentle flow.

The pleasant weather added to our delight as we took in the breathtaking views of the river bed, creating new memories with each passing moment.

As we sat there, I remembered the captivating stories of the Mochi Wala, our childhood friend and masterful tale-spinner. I eagerly asked if anyone would like to share one of his stories, but my mind was already racing with one of my favourites - the tale of the priest who refused to buy sandals.

This enigmatic story has always fascinated me, and I couldn't wait to share it with my friends. The river's soothing ambience and our relaxed mood made it the perfect setting to revisit this childhood classic.With a unanimous vote, I began to recount the story of the priest who refused to buy sandals, a tale that had captivated us for years.

The Priest and The Yakshas

I remember it like yesterday—a lazy Saturday afternoon, where the sun hung lazily in the sky and the day stretched ahead full of promise. School homework was done (well, sort of), and the thrill of freedom was calling our names.

We'd pleaded with our mums to let us out, and after the usual *"Don't be late!"* and *"Stay out of trouble!"*, we were finally off. But to our surprise, most of our friends didn't show up. A no-show! Talk about a let-down.

So, with nothing much to do, we hatched a plan: visit the Mochi Wala. He was always suitable for a tale or two, and we figured his stories could lift our spirits. His shop wasn't far, a little nook tucked between rows of brick houses, smelling faintly of leather and old wood. As we pushed open the creaky door, a familiar sight greeted us—handcrafted sandals and shoes displayed neatly on shelves, their worn-out counterparts waiting in a pile for repairs.

The man was hunched over his workbench, carefully mending a sandal for an elderly lady. His hands moved deftly, stitching with precision from years of practice.

We shuffled in quietly, settling on the long wooden bench along the wall that creaked just enough to make you think twice before leaning back. The shop was dimly lit, the late afternoon sun streaming through the dusty windows. True to his frugal nature, the Mochi Wala didn't bother with the oil lamp unless necessary.

He glanced up and greeted us with a warm smile, his face crinkling like it always did like he had a secret he couldn't wait to share. *"Ah, my young adventurers! Give me a moment to finish this, and we'll chat."*

We sat there, fidgeting, kicking our legs against the bench, surrounded by the smell of leather and the faint tang of glue. The old lady collected her freshly mended sandals and left with a grateful nod, and finally, the Mochi Wala turned his full attention to us.

"So," he said, his grin growing more expansive, *"what brings you a lot here today? Playing hooky from your chores?"*

One of us, bold as brass, piped up, *"We're bored! We thought one of your stories would cheer us up. They're always the best!"*

The rest of us giggled, nodding eagerly. His stories were the stuff of legend—wild, funny, sometimes a bit spooky, but always unforgettable.

His eyes twinkled as he leaned back on his stool, stroking his chin theatrically. *"Bored, are you? Well, lucky for you, I've just the story! It's about a priest who refuses to buy sandals. And let me tell you, his reasoning will leave you in stitches!"*

We perked up immediately, scooting closer, hanging on his every word even before he'd started. The Mochi Wala had that effect—he could make you forget everything else, drawing you into a world that seemed far more magical than the one we lived in.

The little shop seemed to shrink, growing cosier as his voice filled the space. The mix of leather, thread, and sunlight spilling in through the windows created a strangely enchanting atmosphere, like the shop itself was a part of the story.

"So, there was this priest," he began, his tone playful and dramatic. We leaned in even further, our eyes wide, imagining the scene. And just like that, the lazy Saturday afternoon wasn't dull anymore.

It had become one of those moments you'd carry with you forever—the kind that sneaks up on you later in life when you least expect it, filling you with warmth and a little pang of longing.

The Mochi Wala didn't just tell stories; he conjured entire worlds with his words. Each tale was like stepping into a painting brought to life, and as he continued, we were utterly spellbound, hanging on every word.

He leaned forward, his voice conspiratorial, "Now, listen carefully, my young friends. This story is about a peculiar priest named Dasu. He lived in a quaint little village not far from here—a place much like our own. Dasu was a Brahmin, a man of God, revered for his wisdom and devotion. But, he had a trait that made him the talk of the village—he was the stingiest man you'll ever hear of!" We chuckled, intrigued. The Mochi Wala grinned, clearly enjoying our reaction, before carrying on.

"Dasu's frugality wasn't just a quirk but a full-blown obsession. He pinched pennies so hard that you'd swear they screamed. His wife, Lakshmi, a kind-hearted and patient woman, often longed for the simplest pleasures—things most people wouldn't think twice about. And their daughter, Kavita? She was a gem, a proper angel in disguise.

Beautiful, kind, and generous to a fault, she was everything her father was not. The villagers adored her and often said, 'Kavita is a princess trapped in a miser's house.'"

The Mochi Wala paused, letting the weight of Dasu's character sink in.

"Now, Dasu wasn't entirely disliked," he continued. "His devotion to his priestly duties and knowledge of ancient texts made him a respected figure in the village. He rose before dawn every day, performed his rituals by the river, and returned to his barebones home to spend the rest of the day immersed in study or officiating ceremonies.

People sought his blessings and counsel; no function was complete without his presence. But—" he raised a finger for emphasis, "his stinginess was the stuff of legend. The villagers respected him but couldn't help but grumble behind closed doors. 'What good is a priest who won't even give alms to the poor?' they'd say."

We nodded, already imagining the tension between Dasu's reputation and his miserly ways.

"It wasn't just the villagers who suffered from his miserliness," the Mochi Wala added, "oh no, his poor wife and daughter had it far worse. Dasu had just two sets of clothes—one for home and one for ceremonies. 'Why waste money on new clothes when the old ones still cover us?' he'd snap whenever Lakshmi or Kavita dared to ask for something new. Lakshmi eventually gave up asking, but Kavita? She had a rebellious streak in her, that girl."

He paused for dramatic effect, his eyes twinkling.

"And don't get me started on their meals! Plain rice, day in and day out. No spices, no vegetables, no meat. The smell of curries and chapatis wafting from their neighbours' kitchens was the closest thing they had to a feast.

Yet, Dasu had no problem turning up uninvited to village feasts, happily stuffing himself while his wife and daughter sat mortified."

The young waiter burst out laughing. "What a cheeky sod!"

The Mochi Wala nodded, laughing along. "Oh, it gets better. One day, Dasu declared they'd no longer use oil lamps in the evenings. 'The moon is enough light for us,' he said. From then on, the family ate supper before sunset and slept on the rooftop under the moonlight. Romantic, you might think? Not when it's forced upon you every single night!"

"Poor Lakshmi and Kavita. How did they put up with him?"

"With remarkable patience," the Mochi Wala replied. "But even patience has its limits. Kavita, bless her heart, was as generous as her father was stingy. She'd often sneak out to give her belongings to those in need—a scarf to a cold child, a piece of jewellery to a struggling mother.

Dasu hated it, of course, but she didn't care. The villagers adored her for it, calling her the village's 'hidden princess.'"

He leaned in closer, lowering his voice. "Now, one day, a sadhu came to their door, asking for food for his disciples. Kavita, without hesitation, took off her gold necklace—their only valuable possession—and handed it to the sadhu. 'Feed your disciples with this,' she said. The sadhu blessed her and left. But when Dasu found out, you should've seen his face!"

"What did he do?" Viju asked eagerly.

The Mochi Wala smirked. "Dasu went redder than a ripe tomato! He stormed in, shouting, 'You foolish girl! That necklace was our only treasure!' But Kavita? She stood her ground. 'It's just a piece of gold, Baba,' she said. 'People are starving, and you're worried about a necklace?'"

The room fell silent, the weight of Kavita's courage sinking in.

"That, my friends, was the beginning of the end of Dasu's stinginess," the Mochi Wala said with a grin. "But how it all unfolded... well, you'll have to return for that part of the story."

We groaned in protest, but he just laughed, his eyes sparkling with mischief. "Patience, my young ones. Good things come to those who wait."

And just like that, we were hooked, counting down the days until we could return for the next chapter of Dasu's tale.

Kavita's generosity blossomed like a wildflower in spring as the days passed. Her kindness spread through the village, earning her the love of all who knew her. Meanwhile, Dasu's legendary miserliness had turned him into the subject of many whispered conversations. The villagers respected his position but couldn't help rolling their eyes at his extreme penny-pinching ways.

One fateful day, Dasu was invited to a grand village function—a rare event he wouldn't dare miss. Running late, he rushed out of the house, dragging his reluctant disciple along.

As they hurried through the dusty road, Dasu's only pair of sandals—already on their last legs—betrayed him. He tripped on a cluster of pebbles, the flimsy straps snapping apart with a loud *twang*.

"Oh no!" Dasu cried out, staring at his broken sandals as if they were a priceless treasure. "What am I to do now? I can't attend the function barefoot!"

The disciple, ever the dutiful follower, immediately offered his sandals. "Here, Guruji, you can borrow mine."

Dasu, without hesitation, slipped into the disciple's sandals. But true to his miserly nature, he wasn't ready to part with his broken pair. "I can't leave these behind! They're still… fixable," he muttered, cradling the sandals like an injured bird.

The pair looked around and spotted a sprawling banyan tree nearby. "This will do," Dasu declared, placing the broken sandals beneath its shade. "We'll collect them on the way back."

With that, they carried on to the function. Dasu, now comfortably clad in his disciple's sandals, basked in the respect and admiration of the villagers, who greeted him warmly. The event was lively, with music, laughter, and a feast that Dasu enjoyed a little too enthusiastically.

As the sun set, the two set off for home, retracing their steps to the banyan tree. But as they reached the spot, Dasu froze. The sandals were gone.

"Where are they?!" he roared, his voice echoing through the quiet evening air. He scoured the area, lifting branches, peering behind bushes, and even checking up in the tree as if the sandals might have sprouted wings and flown away.

His disciple watched the frantic search with sympathy and suppressed amusement. "Guruji," he ventured cautiously, "perhaps someone took them?"

"Who would steal a broken pair of sandals?!" Dasu shouted, his frustration boiling over. The two spent little daylight combing through the area, but the sandals were nowhere to be found.

As night fell, Dasu begrudgingly gave up. Muttering and grumbling under his breath, he stomped home, still wearing the disciple's sandals. When they reached the house, the disciple stood awkwardly at the door and cleared his throat.

"Ahem, Guruji, might I have my sandals back now?"

Dasu blinked, momentarily startled. "Oh, right," he huffed, pulling them off and shoving them into the disciple's hands. "There. Happy now?"

The disciple wisely chose silence, slipping away into the night, mentally planning to avoid Dasu for the next few days.

At home, Dasu's foul mood hung over the household like a thundercloud. His wife, Lakshmi, tried to comfort him. "You can wear my spare sandals if you like," she offered gently.

"Hmph! As if that'll replace my lost pair," Dasu snapped. He barely touched his dinner, his mind consumed by thoughts of his missing sandals.

That night, he tossed and turned in bed, his mind racing. *"Where could they be? Did someone steal them? What if a mischievous child took them just for a laugh? Or worse, what if they're gone forever?"*

Every creak of the house and rustle of the wind seemed to mock him. By the time the first light of dawn crept over the horizon, Dasu had had enough. He sprang out of bed, barely waiting for the day to break. He skipped breakfast, muttering something about having no appetite, and headed straight for the banyan tree.

The disciple, perhaps out of morbid curiosity or sheer loyalty, joined him without a word. Together, they retraced their steps to the tree, Dasu's bare feet crunching against the dirt road.

As they reached the banyan tree, Dasu's heart pounded with anticipation. His eyes darted around, scanning every inch of the ground.

But there was nothing—no sandals, no sign of them ever having been there.

"No, no, no!" Dasu wailed, throwing his arms in the air. He began searching with renewed desperation, circling the tree and peering into every nook and cranny. The disciple, trying to help, poked around the nearby bushes, but it was no use.

After what felt like hours, Dasu finally slumped, defeated. "They're gone," he whispered, more to himself than anyone else. "My sandals… gone."

The disciple placed a hand on his shoulder. "Perhaps, Guruji, it's time to let them go."

Dasu shot him a glare but said nothing. The two began the long walk back to the village, Dasu's feet bare and his heart heavy with loss.

Back in the village, Dasu wasted no time. He approached nearly everyone he saw, asking the same question with increasing urgency: "Have you seen my sandals? They were broken, left under the banyan tree. Perhaps someone thought they were abandoned?"

The villagers, hiding their amusement, shook their heads one after another. Some tried to keep a straight face, while others exchanged knowing looks. It wasn't long before the whispers started.

"Why's he so obsessed with those old things?" one villager muttered to another.

"Typical Dasu," replied the other, smirking. "He could easily buy new sandals, but he won't spend a penny unless he has to."

A few well-meaning villagers even offered to gift him new sandals. “Priest, please take these. You shouldn’t go barefoot. It’s not proper,” they said, holding out pairs of sturdy, freshly made sandals.

But Dasu waved them off with an air of indignation. “Thank you, but I don’t need new sandals,” he declared. “My old ones can still be repaired. Why waste money on something unnecessary when the ones I had could last for years?”

The villagers, familiar with his frugality, merely nodded and let him be. As Dasu moved on to question another person, a group nearby couldn’t help but chuckle.

“He’s more devoted to those sandals than his morning prayers,” one joked.

“Maybe we should organise a village-wide search party for them,” another grinning.

Meanwhile, Dasu went to the temple with his disciples, hoping a prayer moment might bring him peace. But even here, his thoughts were consumed by his loss. He hurried through his prayers, his lips moving mechanically as his mind wandered back to the banyan tree.

Usually, Dasu took great care in his temple rituals. He offered alms and prasad with genuine gratitude, acknowledging the staff and devotees. But today, he was a different man—distracted and impatient. Without a word, he hastily left the temple, leaving the disciple to step in and make amends quietly.

The disciple approached the staff with a sheepish smile, offering alms on behalf of his mentor. “Apologies,” he said softly. “The priest’s mind is elsewhere today. He…lost something important."

The staff exchanged puzzled looks. "Important? What could be so valuable that he'd forget his duties?" one asked.

Another, catching on, smirked. "It must be those sandals. He's been asking everyone about them."

On their way back, the pair passed the cobbler's shop. Dasu stopped abruptly, his eyes drawn to the display of beautifully crafted sandals. The leather gleamed invitingly in the sunlight, and the intricate stitching spoke of quality and care.

"Oh, how wonderful they look," Dasu thought, his gaze lingering on an excellent pair. He imagined slipping them on momentarily, feeling the soft leather embrace his feet.

The cobbler, noticing Dasu's admiration, approached with a friendly smile. "Priest, you've been looking at these sandals every day. Do you like them? If you do, I can offer you a special price—just for you."

Dasu hesitated, the temptation flickering in his eyes. But then he straightened his back, his frugality taking over. "Thank you for your kindness," he said, "but I'm determined to find my sandals. They're not lost; they're just…temporarily misplaced."

The cobbler chuckled softly as Dasu walked away. "That man has more resolve than sense," he muttered, shaking his head.

Every day, Dasu continued his search, refusing to give up. When he wasn't combing the village or interrogating its residents, he borrowed sandals to get by. Each borrowed pair was a new adventure in discomfort.

Some were so large they flopped with every step, while others were so tight they left marks on his feet. And then there were the mismatched pairs—one green, one brown—that had the village's children giggling every time he walked past.

"Look at the priest's feet!" they whispered, trying not to laugh out loud. "He's got a rainbow on!"

Despite the discomfort and the quiet ridicule, Dasu remained resolute. He passed the cobbler's shop daily, admiring the new sandals before muttering his mantra: "I will find my sandals someday."

One day, as Dasu lingered longer than usual, the cobbler called out to him again. "Priest, these sandals could save you all this trouble. Why not take them? I'll give you the best price in the village."

Dasu smiled faintly, tempted but steadfast. "Thank you, but no. I appreciate your generosity, but my sandals are out there somewhere. I need to find them."

The cobbler watched him walk away, barefoot and determined, shaking his head with amusement and exasperation.

"That man and his sandals," he muttered. "I wonder which will give out first—his resolve or his feet."

Days passed, and the missing sandals became a quiet obsession for Dasu. Then, one day, an invitation to a wedding arrived.

"Ah-ha!" the priest's wife said, a spark of excitement in her voice. This will do us good. It's been far too long since we've attended a proper social event."

"That's so nice! I'm looking forward to it," said Kavita, her eyes lighting up with genuine enthusiasm.

Dasu, however, remained silent. He didn't share their excitement, and his thoughts were elsewhere. But determined to maintain his stature despite the turmoil of his missing sandals, he agreed and set off with his wife and daughter.

The familiar banyan tree loomed as they strolled through the village. Dasu suddenly stopped in his tracks, his expression clouding with melancholy.

"That is where I had kept my broken sandals," he said, pointing at the tree. "I thought I would pick them up on my way home. Alas, I shall never see my sandals again."

His wife gave him a sharp look, raising one eyebrow as if to say, *"Let it go already—don't cry over spilt milk."*

But Kavita's heart softened at her father's apparent sorrow. She nodded solemnly, making a silent promise to herself. "I'll find out what happened to my father's sandals," she thought determinedly.

The following day, Kavita prepared for her mission. Packing some food and water, she headed straight to the banyan tree. She combed through every inch of the area, her hands brushing away dirt and leaves as she checked under roots, behind bushes, and even in the crevices of the tree trunk.

"Hmm, where could it be?" she muttered to herself. "Father asked the villagers, and no one seems to have seen it… so strange."

As the hours dragged on, her energy began to wane. Hunger

gnawed at her, and she finally sat under the tree, unpacking the food her mother had lovingly prepared. Just as she took her first bite, a faint giggling broke the stillness.

Kavita froze, her ears straining. “Who’s there?” she called out, her voice steady despite unease.

No answer came. She looked around but saw nothing—just the swaying branches of the tree and the golden sunlight filtering through the leaves.

Shrugging it off, she resumed eating, but the giggling grew louder, now mixed with bursts of laughter. It seemed to echo from everywhere and nowhere all at once. Her eyes darted upward, scanning the canopy.

“I think I’m hearing things,” she muttered, shaking her head in disbelief.

But then, out of the corner of her eye, something glimmered—a faint shimmer, like sunlight dancing on water. She squinted, trying to focus. Shiny, glowing figures began to materialise in the air around her.

Kavita’s jaw dropped as she stared in wonder. They were delicate, almost translucent, with wings that sparkled like dew-kissed cobwebs in the morning light.

“Yakshas,” she whispered, her breath catching. She remembered her mother’s tales—mythical beings, mischievous and powerful, known to guard treasures and play tricks on humans.

I couldn’t hold back as Mochi Wala narrated this part of the story.

"Wait, Yakshas? What are Yakshas?" I interrupted, leaning forward with curiosity.

The Mochi Wala paused mid-sentence and gave me a stern look. "Don't interrupt me while I'm narrating the story," he said, his tone mock-serious. I might forget what happens next!"

One of my friends let out a snicker. "Someone's touchy about their storytelling!" they teased.

Another chimed in, rubbing their stomach dramatically. "Honestly, all this talk about food has made me starving. Can we take a break?"

I groaned, throwing my hands up in exasperation. "We're almost at the end! Can't you hold on a bit longer?"

It was a majority decision. We drove back to the village and found ourselves in a small, cosy Dhaba. We all sat and had our food, yapped, and giggled. It was a late lunch for us; the story had kept all of us involved, and we forgot about the time.

We decided to sit in the Dhaba and spend the rest of the time listening to the story.

I was about to finish.

Once we were all settled, I continued the story…

"The Mochi Wala seemed troubled because I interrupted him earlier. He looked genuinely flustered as if trying to recollect his thoughts while narrating the tale."

Just as he was about to speak, the tinkling sound of the shop bell interrupted again. A young lady entered, holding a pair of sandals in her hands. She was pretty and confident, and her presence seemed to light up the tiny shop.

"Mochi Ji, could you repair these for me?" she asked, her voice polite yet cheerful.

The Mochi Wala's face broke into a wide smile. "Of course, of course," he said, taking the sandals from her as if they were the most precious thing in the world.

We all exchanged knowing glances, biting back laughter. It was clear as day—he liked her.

As he began mending the sandals, he kept finding excuses to chat. "So, where are you off to in such lovely sandals?" he asked casually, glancing up at her with a grin.

She chuckled softly. "Nowhere fancy. Just thought I'd have them fixed before they fall apart completely."

"Well, they've come to the right place," he said, puffing out his chest slightly. "My hands are the best in the business."

We sat in a quiet huddle, watching the interaction unfold like a scene from a romantic drama. The young lady, clearly enjoying the attention, lingered longer than necessary, her face lighting up with a smile at his every comment.

Finally, with the sandals repaired, she thanked him warmly and left the shop. The moment the door closed behind her, we burst into laughter, unable to contain ourselves any longer.

The Mochi Wala turned to us, his face red with embarrassment and irritation. "What's so funny?" he barked. "Haven't you ever seen a man talking to a woman?"

We laughed, one of us gasping out, "Not like that, Mochi Ji!"

Little did we know that encounter with the young lady would weave itself into our lives in a way we couldn't yet imagine. But I'll save that twist for later in the story.

For now, I tried to steer us back on track. "All right, all right, please continue the story," I said, wiping away tears of laughter. "But first—tell us properly, what *are* Yakshas?"

The Mochi Wala straightened, clearing his throat with an air of importance. "Yakshas," he began, "are a class of supernatural beings. They are protectors of nature and keepers of wealth, often depicted as playful, mischievous creatures. They are known for their love of the natural world, tricks, and deep ties to treasure and secrets."

He paused, looking at us as if waiting for a reaction.

His words, though fascinating, left us scratching our heads. "So... are they good or bad?" one of us asked.

"They're both, depending on their mood," he replied. "Yakshas are neither wholly benevolent nor malicious. They're tricksters, yes, but they also bring blessings. It depends on how you treat them."

This explanation is only half-registered in our minds. We were far more eager to discover what happened next in the story. "All right, Mochi Ji," I said, leaning forward eagerly. "What did the Yakshas do?"

He smiled knowingly as if holding onto a secret we were desperate to uncover. "Ah, patience," he said. "Let me tell you…"

One of the Yakshas, slightly larger than the others, floated down gracefully and hovered in front of Kavita.

"Hello," it said in a melodic voice that seemed to ripple through the air. "We've been watching you. Why are you here?"

Kavita, though startled, gathered her courage. "I'm looking for my father's sandals," she replied earnestly. "He left them here, and they went missing. He's been very upset about it."

The Yaksha tilted its head curiously, then giggled, a playful and otherworldly sound. It turned to the other Yakshas, who also began giggling, their laughter echoing like wind chimes in the breeze.

"If you share the food you've brought with us," said the Yaksha, "we might help you find your father's sandals."

Kavita didn't hesitate. She opened her food box and began handing out portions to the Yakshas. Out of nowhere, two more Yakshas appeared, eagerly joining a feast. They were delighted with her generosity.

"We know you well," said one of the Yakshas between bites, its voice warm and approving. "The villagers speak highly of you."

"Not long ago," added another, "we disguised ourselves as sadhus and came to your home for help. You gave us your gold necklace without a second thought."

“We were so pleased with your kindness,” chimed the third Yaksha.

Kavita smiled softly, but her thoughts quickly returned to her father’s sandals.

The first Yaksha nodded understandingly. “We took the sandals because they intrigued us,” it admitted. “We didn’t mean to cause any harm. Your father is a wise man, but he is also very attached to his possessions.”

Kavita sighed. “Yes, he is. He’s been borrowing sandals from others and is determined to find his own. It would mean a lot to him if he could have them back.”

The Yakshas huddled together, their soft voices buzzing like whispers in the wind. After a moment, they turned back to her.”

We’ll return the sandals,” one said, “but only if you and your father can answer our riddles. If you succeed, the sandals are yours.” Kavita nodded eagerly and ran back home to inform her father. She explained everything—the Yakshas, their mischief, and the challenge they had presented. Though initially sceptical, Dasu agreed, and the family prepared to return to the banyan tree.

When they arrived, the Yakshas were sprawled on the tree branches, snoring softly. Since Kavita had seen them before, they were only visible to her initially. She hesitated, unsure whether waking them would anger them.

She took a deep breath, plucked a large leaf from the ground, and gently fanned the air.

The rustling of the banyan leaves stirred the Yakshas from their slumber. They stretched and yawned, their shimmering forms shifting in the dappled sunlight.

"So, you've returned for your father's broken sandals," said one Yaksha with a teasing grin.

Kavita remained calm. "I'm here with my father, as you requested," she replied confidently. My mother and my father's disciples are also here. They wish to meet you."

The Yakshas seemed pleased with her composure. With a flick of their hands, they revealed their actual forms—majestic, glowing figures with ethereal beauty that seemed to radiate wisdom and mischief.

The group gasped in unison, awestruck by the sight. Kavita's mother stepped forward, her voice trembling with reverence. "Your presence humbles us," she said. "Thank you for granting us this opportunity."

The Yakshas greeted them warmly. "We will ask you three riddles," said the first. "Answer them correctly, and the sandals will be yours."

The first Yaksha stepped forward, its eyes twinkling. "What is more valuable than gold but cannot be bought or sold?"

Kavita furrowed her brow for a moment before answering. "Time. It is precious, and once lost, it can never be regained."

The Yaksha smiled approvingly. "You are correct."

The second Yaksha floated forward, its voice light and playful.

"What is the one thing that travels faster than the wind but has no wings?"

Dasu, the priest, pondered this carefully. After a moment, he replied, "Thought. It can reach anywhere in an instant."

The Yaksha clapped its hands in delight. "You are wise indeed."

Finally, the third Yaksha approached, its tone more solemn. "What is the greatest treasure one can possess yet cannot be seen or touched?"

Kavita and her father exchanged a thoughtful glance. Then, Kavita answered, "Wisdom. It guides us through life and is invaluable."

The Yakshas clapped joyously. "You have answered all our riddles correctly. We are pleased with your wisdom and courage."

With a wave, the Yakshas conjured the missing sandals, now clean and polished, and smiled as they handed them to Kavita.

"These are your father's sandals," one Yaksha said, handing them to Kavita. "We hope they bring him happiness."

Kavita and her family bowed deeply, their hearts brimming with gratitude. As they turned to leave, one of the Yakshas called out, their voice melodic and wise, "Remember, true wealth lies not in possessions but in the wisdom and kindness you share with others."

The words lingered in the air, wrapping around the family like a gentle breeze. Kavita and her family left the forest with a newfound sense of clarity, their minds enriched by the encounter with the mystical beings.

The priest, cradling his sandals like a prized treasure, resolved to have them repaired by the cobbler. Despite their worn-out state, he continued to use them, their presence now a reminder of a profound lesson.

From that day on, the priest transformed. No longer a miser, he began to open his heart and his purse to help the poor and needy. His wife and daughter, once accustomed to his frugality, were surprised and delighted by his newfound generosity.

Kavita's eyes sparkled with joy as her father gave her small but thoughtful gifts, and his wife found herself receiving compliments and tokens of appreciation she had long given up expecting.

The priest's disciples also noticed the change. He became more patient and nurturing, teaching with renewed care. His transformation didn't just stop with his family; it rippled through the village, inspiring others to embrace kindness and generosity. The once sombre village now buzzed with a spirit of togetherness and goodwill, all sparked by the lesson of a lost sandal.

Moral of the story - As the Mochi Wala summed up, the story's moral was simple yet profound: "Material possessions do not measure true wealth, but by the wisdom, kindness, and generosity we share with others. By valuing these qualities, we enrich our lives and the lives of those around us."

With a warm smile, the Mochi Wala concluded, "So, my dear young lads, that was the story of the priest, his wife, and his daughter. The lost sandal was a disguised blessing to teach the priest a valuable lesson.

Through the Yakshas and their riddles, he learned humility, generosity, and the importance of helping others. His transformation brought joy and prosperity to his family and inspired the entire village."

He paused, looking at us with twinkling eyes. "Now go home, and I hope you all liked my story."

We giggled and grinned, reluctant to leave the enchanting little shop. The sun had begun its descent, casting a golden glow over the village. As the shadows lengthened, we said our goodbyes to the Mochi Wala and each other, promising to meet again soon.

On the walk back home, the story stayed with me, its lessons playing repeatedly in my mind. When I reached my doorstep, I felt an overwhelming urge to express my gratitude to my family. I walked straight to my mum and hugged her tightly.

"Thank you, Mum," I said earnestly. "For everything you do—making meals, helping us with our studies, getting us ready for school. You're amazing."

Her eyes widened in surprise, and a smile lit up her face. "Well, this is unexpected! Thank you, my dear," she said, her voice warm with joy.

Next, I found my dad, who was engrossed in his evening paper. "Thank you, Dad," I said, patting his shoulder. "For all your support and guidance. You're the best."

He looked at me over his glasses, clearly taken aback but pleased. "What's gotten into you today?" he chuckled. "But thank you, son."

Lastly, I turned to my siblings. "And thank you too," I said, grinning. "Even though we fight sometimes, you're my best friend."

They stared at me, baffled, before one of them quipped, "You've gone soft!" But I could see they were touched.

That evening, our home was filled with laughter and warmth. For the first time in a long while, I truly appreciated the love and care that bound us together.As I recounted my thoughts to my friends the next day, one of the older lads laughed. "I didn't know you went all emotional after The story! I just went home, stuffed myself with food, and passed out."

Another friend added, "The story was brilliant. I don't think we've ever spent that much time together, just listening without touching our phones."

"Exactly," chimed in someone else. "It felt magical—like we were in another world. The Yakshas, the riddles, the priest's change made me forget everything else."

We all nodded in agreement, realising how rare and unique that moment had been. It wasn't just a story—it was an experience that had connected us, filling us with wonder and a renewed appreciation for the simple joys of life.

Reflective Interlude

"I miss those days when gadgets were not a part of our lives. We only had a TV with limited program timings and only one channel that ran the show. We had to watch whatever was shown, and there was a certain charm in that simplicity," one friend recollected.

"We didn't even have a colour TV and made do with a black-and-white TV for most of our childhoods," added another friend with excitement. "Remember how we used to adjust the antenna to get a clearer picture?"

"Yes! And the whole family would gather around the TV, eagerly waiting for our favourite shows," another friend said. "Those moments felt so special and unifying. There was a certain magic in the anticipation and the shared experience of watching something together."

"Absolutely," the first friend agreed. "Those times were filled with more face-to-face interactions, outdoor play, and a sense of community. We would play outside until dark and then rush home to catch our favourite programs."

"Nowadays, with so many gadgets and endless content at our fingertips, it's easy to feel overwhelmed and disconnected," another friend reflected. "Sometimes, I long for those days' simplicity and genuine connections."

"Me too," the first friend nodded. "There was something so pure about those times. We didn't have the distractions we have now, and it made our interactions more meaningful."

"Exactly," the second friend said. "It's funny how we used to complain about having only one channel, but now I miss it. It made us appreciate what we had and brought us closer together."

Time Capsule - "Guys, it's almost 4:00 PM. Should we call it a day and head back home?" one friend suggested, glancing at his watch.

"It's been a while since we last met. I suggest we stay a bit longer and then decide what we want to do next," another friend replied, clearly enjoying the reunion.

"I'm used to having chai at this hour. If anyone else wants some, we can place the order.

This Dhaba is cosy, I must say," another friend chimed in, looking around appreciatively.

"Do you have any more stories up your sleeves?" one friend asked excitedly. "I haven't had enough of the days of the Mochi Wala."

"Not without ordering chai first! Nothing will get into my head without a chai," grinned one of the more benevolent friends.

"Hahahaha," I laughed. "Let's not keep you waiting for chai. We don't want you to get grumpy."

Another friend suggested, "Meanwhile, someone, please think of the many tales narrated to us by the Mochi Wala. "

"By the way, we must find out what happened to the poor Mochi Wala. We need to know about his whereabouts," one friend added thoughtfully.

"I would love to meet him before we all depart," another inquisitive friend added.

"Agree," we all echoed. We all wanted to meet him.

Newcomer alert - We placed the order for chai and some snacks to go with it. The waiter, a young boy, had been serving us with a shy smile. He was dressed shabbily, his clothes worn and patched, indicating he came from a poor household. It seemed likely that he wasn't attending school, possibly because his family couldn't afford it.

Despite his circumstances, he had a friendly demeanour, his eyes sparkling with curiosity. He had been watching us from a distance, amused by the story of the priest refusing to buy new sandals. He wanted to join us in hearing more such stories. So, I invited him to join us. He was reluctant but finally came over and sat next to us. The boy's hair was neatly combed, but his uniform was slightly oversized and frayed at the edges. As he sat down, he listened intently, clearly fascinated by our conversation.

We waited for the chai and snacks to arrive while we checked our phones for updates and messages, especially from our families. It was a routine that had become second nature to us, a way to stay connected with our loved ones even when we were away.

The notifications and messages brought a sense of closeness, bridging the physical distance. It makes the world feel smaller and more intimate, allowing us to instantly share moments and stay updated on each other's lives.

Despite being engrossed in our digital screens, there was a comfort in knowing that our families were just a message away, ready to share in our joys and concerns. This modern convenience, though often taken for granted, added a layer of connection that complemented our face-to-face interactions.

When the chai finally arrived, the boy carefully placed the cups and saucers in front of us, making sure not to spill a drop. The aroma of freshly brewed chai filled the air, and we all took a moment to savour it. As he served each cup, he said shyly, "Here you go, sir. I hope you enjoy the chai."

We could see the pride in his eyes as he watched us take our first sips. "This is excellent chai," one of us complimented him.

The boy's face lit up with pride. "Thank you, sir. My mother taught me how to make it just right," he said, his voice filled with pride and nostalgia.

"Your mother must be a great trainer," another friend added, smiling warmly.

"Yes, she is," the boy replied, his eyes shining. "She always says that making good chai is an art."

We all nodded in agreement, appreciating the chai and the care and effort that went into making it. The boy lingered for a moment, clearly enjoying the rare praise and the sense of connection with us.

Walk back to memory lane - As we sipped our chai, the conversation drifted back to the past. "Remember how we used to play outside until it got dark?" one friend recalled. "We'd rush home just in time to catch our favourite TV shows."

"Yes, and we only had one channel!" another friend laughed. "We had to watch whatever was on, but it made those moments special."

"Those were the days," I said, smiling. "We didn't have all these gadgets, but we had each other. There was a certain magic in the simplicity of it all."

"Absolutely," another friend agreed. "Nowadays, with so many gadgets and endless content at our fingertips, it's easy to feel overwhelmed and disconnected. Sometimes, I long for those days' simplicity and genuine connections."

The young waiter listened intently, his eyes wide with curiosity. "It sounds like you all had much fun back then," he said softly.

"We did," one friend replied warmly. "And it's moments like these, sharing stories and enjoying each other's company, that remind us of how important those times were."

We all nodded in agreement, feeling a deep nostalgia and appreciation for the past. The chai and snacks perfectly accompanied our reflective interlude, making the moment even more special.

"I would surely want to be part of another story telltale, please," he pleaded.

"We have time for at least one more story shared by our beloved Mochi Wala," I said, smiling at the boy's enthusiasm. "There are many folktales he shared with us. It's difficult even to pick which one was our favourite."

"I have one which is quite interesting and one of the favourites of our beloved Mochi Wala."

Immediately, all my friends gathered around me, holding chai and snacks.

"Hope it's the story of the tone-deaf Singer," cried out one of the friends.

"Please bear with me," I replied.

The Cobblers Magical Wallet

Many years ago, in a quiet little village just a day's ride from King Aditya's bustling capital, there lived a cobbler named Amsula and his fiery wife, Meera. Amsula was a craftsman through and through, known far and wide for his impeccable leather goods—shoes that fit like a dream, wallets that lasted a lifetime, and sandals that were as sturdy as they were comfortable.

He was humble, soft-spoken, and kind-hearted, the sort of person everyone in the village trusted. Have you got a sandal strap snapped on your way to the market? Amsula would fix it without charging you a single coin. Is your wallet falling apart? He'd repair it for next to nothing. That's just how he was. The villagers adored him, preferring his honest services over the fancy cobblers in the capital who charged an arm and a leg.

But for all his charm and goodwill, Amsula had a challenge waiting for him every evening—his wife, Meera. Don't get me wrong; Meera wasn't a bad person. She loved her husband in her way. But she had a temper that could shake the walls, and she wasn't shy about letting Amsula know precisely what she thought of his "ridiculous pricing."

"Why do you charge so little?!" she'd snap when he stepped through the door. "Do you think we can survive on your generosity? People in this village would pay more if you asked! You're the only cobbler for miles, Amsula!"

Amsula would smile, hanging up his bag of tools. "It's not about the money, Meera," he'd say calmly, his tone almost rehearsed. "People come to me because they trust me, not because I overcharge them."

"Trust doesn't put food on the table!" Meera would huff, arms crossed, tapping her foot impatiently.

And so it went, day after day, their little tug-of-war over money. Amsula never lost his temper, no matter how fiery Meera got. He'd nod, sit down to his dinner, and let her words roll off him like water off a duck's back.

Now, Meera wasn't just angry for the sake of it. She had her reasons. Life wasn't exactly a picnic for the couple. While Amsula's reputation made him beloved, it didn't do much to line their pockets. Every day, he'd come home with a modest handful of coins—just enough to scrape by.

And oh, how Meera guarded those coins. The moment Amsula walked in, she'd take whatever he'd earned, tucking it away in her tightly controlled stash. If Amsula needed a coin for himself—even for something as small as a cup of chai—he'd have to ask her, and she didn't make it easy.

"What do you need it for?" she'd demand, eyebrows raised. "Is it urgent?"

"Just a chai, Meera," he'd reply patiently. "I've been on my feet all day."

"Hmm," she'd say, eyeing him suspiciously before begrudgingly handing over a single coin. "Don't waste it!"

Amsula, for his part, didn't mind too much. He'd learned to live, finding joy in his work and the trust of his neighbours. But deep down, he sometimes wished Meera could see the world like he did—that helping people was worth more than gold.

The villagers, of course, knew about Meera's temper. Some even teased Amsula about it when they came to his shop.

"Cobbler, does your wife know you're giving me a discount?" one cheeky farmer asked, grinning as Amsula repaired his torn sandal.

Amsula chuckled, shaking his head. "She'll find out eventually," he said, his tone light.

"She's a tough one, your Meera," the farmer said, clapping Amsula on the back. "But you've got a heart of gold, my friend. Don't let her wear you down."

And he didn't. No matter how much Meera grumbled, Amsula stuck to his principles. He believed that his craft was about more than just making money—it was about serving the community, about being the kind of person people could rely on.

But life in the village was far from predictable, and little did Amsula know that his quiet existence was about to take a turn. This twist would test his patience, kindness, and perhaps even Meera's fiery resolve.

Unbeknownst to Amsula, the humble cobbler of the village, a group of mystical elves lived deep in the enchanted forest nearby. These weren't your average, mischievous garden-variety elves—they were ancient beings, guardians of the forest, and protectors of those with pure hearts. They had been silently watching Amsula for years, impressed by his craftsmanship and moved by his selflessness.

"What a kind soul," one elf murmured as they observed Amsula repairing a child's worn-out sandal for free.

"Yes," another agreed, their voice like the chiming of bells. "But his wife is another story."

The elves were saddened by Amsula's plight, especially how Meera controlled every coin he earned, leaving him with little for himself. They decided it was time to intervene.

One moonlit night, as the village lay under a blanket of stars, the elves visited Amsula in his dreams. Their forms shimmered like starlight, and their leader, Elowen, stepped forward. Her voice was soft yet commanding, like the rustling of leaves on a breezy night.

"Amsula," she said, her ethereal gaze meeting his, "your kindness and skill have not gone unnoticed. You give so much and ask for so little in return. We wish to help you."

Amsula blinked in surprise. "Help me? But… how?"

Elowen smiled. "We will teach you to craft a magical wallet. This wallet will have secret pockets, invisible to anyone but you. It can hide anything—money, trinkets, even your thoughts if you wish—and no one else can ever detect them."

Amsula listened intently, his heart swelling with gratitude. Before he could respond, the dream faded, and he awoke to the first light of dawn streaming through his small window.

The elves' guidance was vividly remembered, and for the first time in ages, Amsula felt a spark of excitement. He wasted no time, heading to his shop with a renewed sense of purpose.

The elves had told him about a rare material called Moonshadow leather, harvested from deer that roamed the enchanted forest under the full moon. He had some scraps tucked away—a gift from a traveller who had traded it for repairs long ago. Amsula had always thought it too beautiful to use, but now it seemed like fate.

The leather shimmered like liquid silver under his touch, and as he worked, he felt a strange energy radiating from it. He stitched and folded with meticulous care, following the instructions from his dream. Every move felt guided, like the elves were still watching over him.

By the time he finished, the wallet was unlike anything he'd ever seen. Its surface gleamed with an otherworldly sheen, and the secret pockets were so cleverly hidden that they seemed to defy reality. He tested it immediately, slipping in a few coins and a small trinket. They vanished as though swallowed by the wallet, reappearing when he willed them back.

"Brilliant," he muttered, a rare grin spreading across his face.

That evening, Amsula returned home, the magical wallet tucked safely in his bag. As usual, Meera was waiting for him at the door, arms crossed and a suspicious look on her face.

"Hand it over," she said curtly, holding her hand.

Amsula complied, placing the wallet in her palm with an innocent expression. Meera opened it immediately, her sharp eyes scanning for every coin and note.

But something was off.

"Where's the rest of it?" she demanded, her tone already accusatory.

"That's all I earned today," Amsula replied calmly, watching her with barely concealed amusement.

Meera scowled, pulling at the wallet's seams, searching every corner. No matter how hard she tried, she couldn't find the hidden compartments. "This is strange," she muttered, her frustration growing. "How do you seem to be making less money these days?"

Amsula shrugged, fighting back a smirk. "Business has been a bit slow," he said, his tone perfectly innocent.

Meera huffed, snapping the wallet shut. "Useless," she grumbled, storming off to count the visible coins.

As she disappeared into the next room, Amsula allowed himself a small chuckle. He felt a sense of quiet triumph for the first time in years. The wallet wasn't just a tool—it was freedom.

…I was interrupted by the young waiter. "I found a wallet a long time ago. I haven't used it and kept it in my closet," he said. "It's quite old and worn out. Maybe it's magical. I need to test it."

We all started laughing; it sounded so hilarious. The silence was broken when one of my dear friends commented, "I wish I had such a magical wallet. I could hide my money from my wife." We all chuckled loudly.

"Shall we take a break and enjoy these sudden outburst moments?" I added.

The young waiter was eager to hear the story. The magical wallet story fascinated him. "Please continue the story. I want to know what happened next," he said excitedly.

"Please sit tight and hear me out without any more intermissions."

Amsula, meanwhile, felt a quiet satisfaction. Thanks to the mystical elves' kindness and Moonshadow Leather's magic, he had found a way to keep some of his hard-earned money for himself for the first time in years. He carried on with his work, crafting more magical wallets, always careful to keep his secret safe. His cheerful demeanour was far from the burdened and dejected Amsula the villagers once knew.

His grin was wide enough to rival the sun when he strolled through the village. He greeted everyone with a warm smile, a friendly nod, or a quick joke that left them chuckling. The villagers couldn't help but notice the change.

"What's gotten into him?" whispered one woman to her neighbour as Amsula passed by. "I've never seen him so... happy!"

"Maybe Meera's finally lightened up," her neighbour replied with a wink, setting them both off into peals of laughter.

One sunny afternoon, while Amsula was busy stitching a particularly tricky repair, his close friend Bhaswar stopped by the shop. Bhaswar had been observing Amsula's transformation for weeks and could no longer contain his curiosity.

"Amsula, my old mate," Bhaswar began, pulling up a stool. You look like a man with a weight lifted off his shoulders. What's your secret? You have found a pot of gold, have you?"

Amsula hesitated, caught off guard. He had promised himself he'd keep the magical wallet a secret. Still, something about Bhaswar's eager face and long-standing friendship made him falter.

"Well... it's not exactly gold," Amsula admitted, lowering his voice as he leaned closer. "It's a magical wallet."

Bhaswar blinked. "A what now?"

"A magical wallet," Amsula repeated, glancing around to ensure no one else was listening. "The elves of the enchanted forest taught me how to make it. It's got secret pockets where I can hide money and valuables. Meera can't find a thing, no matter how hard she looks!"

For a moment, Bhaswar said nothing, his expression frozen in disbelief. Then he burst out laughing. "Elves? Magical wallets? You've been working too hard, mate!"

Amsula, unfazed, pulled out the wallet crafted from the shimmering Moonshadow Leather. "Laugh all you like, but watch this."

He slipped a few coins and a small trinket into the wallet. With a flick of his fingers, the items disappeared as if they had never existed. Then, just as effortlessly, he retrieved them, holding them up with a triumphant grin.

Bhaswar's laughter stopped mid-chuckle. His jaw dropped. "By the gods… it's real!" he exclaimed, his voice barely above a whisper.

"Of course, it's real," Amsula grinned.

"You've got to make me one, Amsula!" Bhaswar said, his eyes gleaming with excitement.

"I will," Amsula promised. "But you've got to keep it a secret. This is a gift from the elves, and it's not to be taken lightly. Promise me, Bhaswar."

"You have my word," Bhaswar said, his tone solemn.

That night, however, Bhaswar couldn't stop thinking about the magical wallet. The image of the shimmering leather, the secret pockets, and the way the coins vanished were all too fascinating. Even in his sleep, his excitement spilled over.

"Mmm… magical wallet… secret pockets…" he murmured in his dreams.

His wife, a light sleeper with ears sharper than a fox's, woke up instantly. The following day, arms crossed, she asked, demanding answers, "What's this about a magical wallet?"

Bhaswar, caught off guard and groggy from sleep, stammered, "Uh… nothing! It's just a dream, that's all."

"Oh, no, you don't," she said, narrowing her eyes. "You're terrible at lying, Bhaswar. Tell me the truth."

Realising he had no way out, Bhaswar sighed and spilt everything—Amsula's magical wallet, the elves, the secret pockets. His wife listened, her eyes widening with every word.

"We have to see this wallet!" she declared.

"No, no, I promised Amsula I wouldn't tell anyone," Bhaswar protested weakly.

"Well, you've already told me," she shot back. "And I'm not just anyone."

Before he could argue further, she was already halfway out the door, dragging him along.

When they arrived at Amsula's shop, the cobbler looked up from his work, his face breaking into a smile. But he sighed when he saw the curious glint in Bhaswar's wife's eyes.

"So much for keeping a secret," Amsula said, shaking his head.

Bhaswar shuffled awkwardly. "I'm sorry, mate. She overheard me in my sleep."

Amsula chuckled despite himself. "I should've known better. Come in, then. Let me show you."

He retrieved the magical wallet and demonstrated its properties once more. Bhaswar's wife watched, utterly captivated, as the items disappeared and reappeared like magic.

"This is incredible," she whispered, her voice filled with awe. "You're sitting on a fortune, Amsula! You could sell these for a king's ransom!"

"Maybe," Amsula replied, tucking the wallet away, "but it's not about the money. This is about balance—keeping a little for myself while helping those who need it. That's what the elves wanted."

Bhaswar's wife left the shop with stars in her eyes, already planning how to tell her friends about the magical wallet. Amsula could only sigh, knowing his secret wouldn't stay hidden for long.

But deep down, he wasn't too worried. After all, kindness and wisdom, like magic, were meant to be shared.

And so, the word of Amsula's magical wallets spread like wildfire through the village and far beyond. Men from neighbouring hamlets and distant towns began seeking him out, eager to own one of his enchanted creations.

"These wallets are lifesavers," whispered one villager to another at the market. "Amsula's craftsmanship is unmatched! You can hide anything in those secret pockets—money, jewels, even the odd biscuit if you fancy."

Another chuckled. "My wife hasn't caught on yet. She still thinks

I barely make a coin!"

Men from far and wide came to Amsula, desperate for wallets to keep their hard-earned money safe from prying eyes—or, more often, controlling spouses. True to his kind-hearted nature, Amsula never refused anyone. He carefully crafted each wallet, ensuring the secret pockets were perfectly concealed, just as the elves had taught him.

It wasn't long before the tale of Amsula's magical wallets reached the palace of King Aditya himself. The usually stoic courtroom was abuzz with whispers about the cobbler and his extraordinary skills. Ministers exchanged hushed conversations, courtiers leaned in to gossip, and even the palace guards couldn't help but join in.

The King, seated on his gilded throne, noticed the commotion and frowned. "What's all this murmuring about?" he demanded, his voice echoing through the grand hall. "Am I not to be included in this fascinating discussion?"

One of the ministers stepped forward, clearing his throat nervously. "Your Majesty, we have heard of a cobbler named Amsula, who resides in a small village nearby. It is said that he crafts magical wallets with secret pockets that conceal anything, no matter how big or small."

King Aditya raised an eyebrow, his expression a mix of astonishment and scepticism. "Magical wallets, you say? Are you hiding anything at all? It sounds like the stuff of children's tales."

The minister nodded earnestly. "Indeed, Sire, but the rumours are persistent. Men from across the region swear by his skill."

The King leaned back on his throne, stroking his beard thoughtfully. "If there is truth to this, I must see it for myself. Summon this cobbler to the palace immediately!"

A soldier and the King's trusted advisor were dispatched at once, their boots echoing as they marched through the palace gates and into the village. When they arrived at Amsula's humble shop, the cobbler was busy stitching a pair of sandals for a farmer.

The soldier handed Amsula a rolled parchment sealed with the royal insignia. "Amsula the cobbler," he announced, his tone commanding, "by order of His Majesty, King Aditya, you are summoned to the royal court. You must appear without delay."

Amsula's hands trembled as he accepted the summons. His heart sank, his mind racing with worry. "Why would the King want to see me?" he murmured. "Have I done something wrong? Will I be punished for the magic of the wallet?"

The advisor, noticing his fear, placed a reassuring hand on his shoulder. "Do not fret, cobbler. His Majesty is a fair and just ruler. Speak the truth, and you will have nothing to fear."

With a heavy heart, Amsula gathered the magical wallet and prepared to journey to the palace.

As Amsula approached the grand palace gates, he felt awe and trepidation. The towering walls, the intricate carvings, and the sheer opulence overwhelmed him. He had never set foot in such a grand space before.

The soldiers at the gate escorted him through the palace's lavish

halls, their polished armour gleaming under the sunlight streaming through stained-glass windows. Amsula clutched the magical wallet tightly, silently praying to the elves that their gift would not trouble him. When they reached the courtroom, Amsula was ushered in. The sight before him was breathtaking—the regal throne, the towering columns, and the richly woven tapestries adorned the walls. King Aditya sat at the centre, surrounded by his ministers and courtiers, his presence commanding and regal.

Amsula bowed deeply, his voice trembling as he spoke. "Your Majesty, I am Amsula, the cobbler you summoned."

The King regarded him with a curious gaze. "Rise, Amsula," he said, his tone firm yet not unkind. "I have heard much about you and your so-called magical wallets. Tell me—are the rumours true?"

Amsula hesitated, unsure how much to reveal. "Your Majesty," he began cautiously, "I am a humble cobbler. My wallets, indeed, have… unique qualities. They were crafted with knowledge given to me in a dream."

The courtroom erupted in murmurs, the ministers exchanging incredulous glances. The King raised a hand to silence them. "A dream, you say? And what knowledge is this?"

Amsula swallowed hard, then took a deep breath. "The secret of creating hidden pockets, invisible to all but the owner," he explained. "With respect, Your Majesty, I can demonstrate if you wish."

King Aditya leaned forward, his curiosity piqued. "Show me."

Amsula carefully unwrapped the wallet, which was made of shimmering Moonshadow leather. He placed a coin and a ring inside and then carefully closed it. When he opened it again, both items were gone.

The King's eyes widened in astonishment. "Where are they?"

Amsula reached into one of the hidden compartments and retrieved the items, presenting them to the King. Gasps filled the courtroom as the ministers leaned in for a closer look.

"Incredible," the King murmured, examining the wallet with great interest. "This is no ordinary craftsmanship."

"Your Majesty," Amsula said humbly, "this wallet is a gift of kindness meant to help those in need. It is not for power or greed." King Aditya's eyes widened in astonishment, his scepticism melting like morning dew under the sun. "This is truly remarkable," he said, leaning forward on his throne. "Tell me, Amsula, how did you come by such a wondrous creation?"

Amsula took a deep breath, his voice steady despite the grandeur of the royal court. "Your Majesty, the knowledge was a gift from the elves of the enchanted forest. They appeared to me in a dream and shared their wisdom. This wallet, crafted from Moonshadow Leather, is imbued with their magic. It is not just my skill, but their blessing, that makes it extraordinary."

The King listened intently, his expression softening as Amsula spoke. By the time the tale was finished, he was thoroughly convinced. He looked down at the humble cobbler with something akin to respect.

"You are a man of great humility and kindness," King Aditya said, reverberating through the hall. "But let us put this magical wallet to the ultimate test." He rose from his throne, the room falling silent in anticipation. "Amsula, I have a task for you—life and death."

Amsula's heart thudded in his chest as the King continued. "Our neighbouring Kingdom is suffering from famine and drought. Their King has pleaded for our help. We must send gold coins and food rations to aid them. However, there is a risk—our enemies may intercept the supplies and steal the gold and food before they reach our allies. This cannot be allowed to happen."

The King's piercing gaze met Amsula's. "You must use your magical wallet to transport these supplies safely and undetected. Are you up to the challenge, Amsula?"

The cobbler bowed deeply, his hands trembling slightly. "Yes, Your Majesty. I will do my best," he said, his voice steady but his heart filled with apprehension.

As he left the courtroom, Amsula's mind raced. How could a simple cobbler like him undertake such a monumental task? Could the wallet handle the treasure and rations required to save an entire Kingdom? The weight of responsibility bore down on him, and his anxiety grew with every step.

Accompanied by the King's trusted adviser and a group of soldiers, Amsula set off toward the palace's secret vaults. They ventured into a secluded area, their path leading to a shadowy cave.

The journey was treacherous. The narrow passages twisted and turned, the jagged rocks underfoot threatening to trip them at every step. The flickering torchlight cast eerie shadows, and the air grew colder and damper with each passing moment.

"This way," the adviser said, echoing through the cavern.

Amsula followed, his palms sweaty as he clutched the magical wallet. The oppressive silence was broken only by the drip of water and the rhythmic sound of their footsteps. His heart pounded in his chest, each step heavier than the last.

Finally, they reached an ancient wooden door reinforced with iron. The adviser produced a large, ornate key and turned it in the lock with a loud clunk. The soldiers pushed the door open, and Amsula gasped at what lay before him.

The vault was vast, its walls lined with gold, jewellery, and precious gems. Piles of coins sparkled in the dim torchlight, their brilliance almost blinding. But alongside the treasure lay barrels and sacks of food—grains, dried fruits, and other essentials for the famine-stricken Kingdom.

Amsula's mouth went dry. How was he supposed to fit all this into the magical wallet? His hands trembled as he approached the piles of gold and supplies. He could feel the weight of the soldiers' and adviser's eyes on him, their expressions a mix of scepticism and expectation.

"Go on, then," the adviser said, his tone challenging. "Show us the magic."

As Amsula hesitated, beads of sweat forming on his brow, a faint shimmer appeared in the corner of his vision. He glanced around nervously, but the soldiers didn't seem to notice. Then, as if stepping out of the shadows, the elves materialised before him.

Their leader, Elowen, smiled reassuringly. “Do not fear, Amsula. You have done well to carry this burden. We will help you now.”

Amsula’s shoulders sagged in relief as the elves began casting their magic. Their hands moved gracefully, and with each motion, the chests of gold and sacks of grain began to shrink and disappear into the wallet’s hidden compartments. Amsula felt the wallet grow slightly heavier in his hands, but its size remained the same.

“Thank you,” he whispered, his voice trembling with gratitude.

The elves smiled and disappeared as silently as they had come, leaving Amsula to face the soldiers and adviser.

The adviser stepped closer, peering at the now-full wallet with suspicion. “You’ve done well so far,” he admitted, though his tone remained guarded. “But the King will not be so easily convinced. Your task is not complete, cobbler. You must deliver these supplies safely to the neighbouring Kingdom.”

Amsula nodded, his heart pounding like a war drum. He knew the real challenge lay ahead. The once scenic journey through rolling meadows, towering mountains, and rugged terrain felt daunting and ominous as the group set off toward the neighbouring Kingdom. The weight of their mission bore down on him, and every step felt heavier than the last.

The soldiers marched in disciplined silence, their faces unreadable masks of determination. Amsula trudged beside the adviser, clutching the magical wallet in his pocket like a talisman. Despite the crisp morning air, beads of sweat gathered at his temples. He glanced nervously at the soldiers, trying to gauge their mood.

One of them, a grizzled man with a scar across his cheek, broke the silence. "So, cobbler," he said with a half-smile, "is this magical wallet of yours the real deal? Or are we just risking our necks for a fancy leather?"

Amsula managed a nervous chuckle. "It's real enough," he replied, his voice shaky. "It saved us all back in the dungeons, didn't it?"

The soldier smirked. "Fair point. Let's hope it pulls another miracle if we need it."

The adviser, walking ahead, glanced back. "Keep your wits about you," he said curtly. "This isn't the place for idle chatter."

They pressed on, the air growing heavier with tension as they approached a notorious passageway flanked by sheer rock walls. The lead soldier raised his hand to halt the group. "Stay sharp," he warned. "This passage is infamous for ambushes. Raiders and bandits love to prey on those foolish enough to carry valuables through here."

The group instinctively tightened their formation, their senses on high alert. Amsula felt a chill run down his spine as every shadow held hidden threats. The oppressive silence was broken only by the occasional clink of armour and the soft crunch of boots on gravel.

Suddenly, a cry pierced the air, and raiders erupted from the shadows, their crude weapons gleaming in the dim light. The soldiers formed a defensive circle but were quickly overwhelmed by sheer numbers. Amsula felt rough hands grab him, and within moments, they were all bound and blindfolded.

As they stumbled along, Amsula could hear the raiders muttering amongst themselves. He strained to catch snippets of their conversation, his fear mingling with a desperate need to stay alert.

When the blindfolds were removed, they found themselves in a cavern dimly lit by torches. The gang's leader sat on a throne of stolen treasures, his scarred face a mask of disdain. He studied them with cold, calculating eyes before barking, "Who dares trespass through my territory? Speak, or you'll regret it!"

Amsula's mouth went dry, but he forced himself to respond. "We mean no harm, sir. We were banished from the Kingdom… for carrying this cursed wallet."

The leader's eyes narrowed. "Cursed? What nonsense is this?"

The adviser stepped forward, his tone smooth. "It's true. This cobbler's wallet brought misfortune upon the King and his court. We were ordered to escort him out of the Kingdom to rid it of its bad luck."

The gang leader snorted, clearly unconvinced. "Show me this so-called cursed wallet."

One of the raiders handed it to him, and the leader turned it over in his hands, inspecting its craftsmanship. "Doesn't look cursed to me," he muttered, his tone mocking. "Feels like fine leather."

Amsula, his mind racing, took a bold step forward. "It's not the leather that's cursed," he said, his voice trembling but firm. "It's what lies within. Anyone who keeps it for too long suffers great misfortune."

The gang leader froze, his expression shifting from amusement to unease. He tossed the wallet onto the ground as if it had burned him, then wiped his hands furiously on his tunic. "Take it and go!" he roared. "I want nothing to do with your cursed belongings!"

The soldiers exchanged astonished glances as the raiders shoved them out of the cavern, their belongings hastily returned. Amsula bent down to pick up the wallet, his hands shaking with relief.

The grizzled soldier clapped Amsula on the shoulder as they returned to the path. "You've got a sharp tongue, cobbler. Saved our hides back there."

Another soldier chuckled. "Who knew a cobbler could outwit a gang of raiders? Maybe we should hire you as a strategist."

The adviser nodded, his expression softening. "You've proven yourself resourceful, Amsula. The King will be pleased to hear of your quick thinking."

Amsula offered a faint smile though his heart was still racing. "I just did what I had to," he said modestly.

Tension eased as they resumed their journey, and the once ominous landscape felt like a sanctuary. When they finally arrived at the neighbouring Kingdom, the sight of the gold coins and food rations brought visible relief to its officials. They welcomed the group with open arms, their gratitude evident in their warm smiles and kind words.

As Amsula handed over the wallet containing the supplies, he couldn't help but feel a swell of pride. He had faced danger, outwitted bandits, and fulfilled his duty. Moved by the story of their journey, the officials offered the group a feast and a place to rest, their hospitality a balm for the weary travellers.

The magical wallet, the elves' gift, had saved him and many others. And though the road ahead was still uncertain, he knew he had the courage and ingenuity to face whatever challenges came his way.

"This is a blessing," one of the officials exclaimed, his eyes brimming with gratitude. "Your King has shown great kindness, and we are forever in his debt."

The team carefully accounted for every last coin and grain before handing over the supplies. Amsula couldn't help but feel a swell of pride as he watched the officials inspect the goods.

After the formalities were complete, they were offered a place to rest. "You must be exhausted from your journey," said a kind-hearted official. "Please, take some time to recover."

The group was led to modest but comfortable quarters, where they finally could wash off the road's dust. The sight of a hearty meal waiting for them brought smiles all around—steaming rice, fragrant curry, and freshly baked bread that filled the room with an inviting aroma.

"This feels like a feast fit for a king," one of the soldiers said, digging in with gusto.

"Better than the dry rations we've been surviving on," added another, his grin widening.

Even Amsula, usually reserved, allowed himself to relax. The warmth of the food and the hospitality of the Kingdom were a welcome relief after their harrowing journey.

Once rested and rejuvenated, the group prepared for their return journey. "We'll take a different route this time," the adviser announced, rolling out a map. "It's longer but avoids the passage where we were ambushed."

Everyone nodded in agreement. Safety was a priority, even if it meant extra travel days.

The new path led them through tranquil landscapes—a patchwork of lush meadows, quiet villages, and winding rivers. The air was filled with the scent of wildflowers, and the only sounds were birdsong and the rustle of leaves in the breeze. This starkly contrasted the tension of their earlier journey, and Amsula reflected on everything they had endured.

"Funny, isn't it?" one of the soldiers remarked as they trudged along. "A magical wallet, a gang of raiders, and now this peaceful stroll. Feels like something out of a bard's tale."

Amsula chuckled, though he felt a pang of nervousness. "Let's just hope the story ends on a good note," he replied.

When they finally reached their Kingdom, Amsula was immediately summoned to the grand hall. The King sat tall on his throne, his expression unreadable. Beside him, the Queen watched with a mix of hope and doubt. The hall was packed with courtiers and villagers, their hushed whispers creating a buzz of anticipation.

The adviser stepped forward, recounting the journey in vivid detail. He described the ambush, Amsula's clever ruse, and the successful delivery of the supplies. With each word, the crowd leaned in closer, their faces a mixture of awe and admiration.

When the tale concluded, the King stood, his stern face breaking into a rare smile. "You have done the impossible, Amsula," he declared, his voice ringing through the hall. "Your bravery, wit, and skill have brought honour to our Kingdom."

The crowd erupted into applause, the sound echoing off the high ceilings.

"You have a rare gift," the King continued, his tone softer now. "And you have used it wisely. From this day forward, you shall be known as the Royal Cobbler. You will craft all the leather goods for the palace, and your name will be celebrated far and wide."

Amsula bowed deeply, overwhelmed by the King's praise. "Thank you, Your Majesty," he said, his voice thick with emotion. "I am honoured beyond words."

Life changed swiftly for Amsula. As the Royal Cobbler, he moved into a comfortable home near the palace. Orders for his magical wallets poured in, not just from the Kingdom but from far-off lands. Yet, despite his growing fame and wealth, Amsula remained humble.

He never forgot the kindness of the elves. Every month, without fail, he left a pair of finely crafted shoes at the edge of the enchanted forest as a token of gratitude.

The elves, though unseen, continued to watch over him. Their presence was felt in the gentle rustle of the trees, the sparkle of morning dew, and the occasional whisper of the wind. They ensured that Amsula's life remained prosperous and peaceful, their bond a symbol of harmony between humans and the mystical beings of the forest.

Amsula's story spread across the land, becoming a tale of inspiration. Villagers spoke of the humble cobbler who turned a Magical gift into a force for good. Children grew up hearing about his bravery and kindness, and travellers shared the legend in distant markets and taverns.

And so, Amsula, who once had little more than his skill and a kind heart, became a legend. His life was a testament to the power of humility, gratitude, and wise choices.

Moral of the story - The story of Amsula and his magical wallet reminds us that material possessions don't measure true wealth. It lies in the kindness we show, the wisdom we share, and the gratitude we carry in our hearts.

"Now that," one of the soldiers said as they toasted Amsula at a feast in his honour, "is a tale worth telling for generations."

And with that, the cobbler's name was etched into the annals of history—a reminder that even the simplest among us can achieve greatness with the right heart and a touch of magic.

Au Revoir

I was knackered from spinning story after story for my friends and the young waiter who'd somehow become one of us in just a few hours. My throat was dry, my voice nearly gone, and I was sure I didn't have it in me to tell another tale.

But my friends? Oh no, they were still going strong, absolutely excited, and obsessed with the magical wallet.

One of them laughed, their eyes sparkling with nostalgia. "We do miss the Mochi Wala, don't we? He was our childhood hero! Those folktales of his might sound proper now, but back then, they felt like gospel truth. We believed every word!" Another friend, leaning back with a wistful grin, chimed in. "Honestly, those were the best days of our lives. No phones, no gadgets—just us and our wild imaginations.

We'd have missed it all if we'd had tech back then. Can you even imagine?"

I glanced at my watch, which read nearly 6:00 p.m. The responsible side of me took over. "All right, gang," I said, clapping my hands together. Let's call it a day. We've all got places to be."

The young waiter, who had somehow transitioned from serving us tea to being part of our crew, got hugs and pats on the back as we said our goodbyes. There were promises to stay in touch, and the usual was, "Until next time!" But as we each headed our separate ways, one thought lingered in the air like a heavy mist: the Mochi Wala.

It was sad. Thinking about how much he'd meant to us, how much his stories had shaped our childhoods, and yet knowing we might never see him again. Where could he be now? Was he still in the same place, spinning tales for another group of wide-eyed kids? Or had time swept him away, as it tends to do? As I made my way home, the weight of nostalgia pressing down on me like a comforting blanket, these questions swirled in my mind.

As I drove, Mochi Wala's tales replayed in my head like an old film reel—stories brimming with adventure, wonder, and life lessons that seemed monumental back then. I could almost see us as kids huddled around him, hanging on to every twist and turn of his narratives. His rich, warm voice transported us to far-off lands where the impossible became possible.

Tonight had been no different. The magical wallet story had unlocked a treasure trove of memories. We'd laughed until our sides ached, recounting how we used to act out his stories. One of us always volunteered to be the dashing hero while the rest played villains or cheered from the sidelines. It was all so wonderfully uncomplicated back then.

When I pulled up to my house and stepped out of the car, I lingered on the pavement momentarily. The cool evening breeze brushed against my face as I looked at the darkening sky. How much had changed since those carefree days? We'd grown up, taken on responsibilities, and moved forward. Yet, the Mochi Wala had left an indelible mark on all of us.

I couldn't shake the thought of finding him again. The idea filled me with an unexpected sense of hope and excitement. Surely, someone in our old neighbourhood would know where he'd gone? I made a mental note to bring it up with the others the next time we met. The thought of sitting with him once more, listening to one of his magical tales, felt like a joy worth chasing.

As I stepped inside my home, the familiar scent of dinner wafting through the air, a smile crept across my face. The evening had been perfect—full of laughter, cherished memories, and a glimmer of something more.

And that magical wallet wasn't just a silly story. Perhaps it was a sign—a gentle nudge to remind us that the magic we believed in as kids wasn't gone. It was still there, patiently waiting for us to rediscover it.I resolved to hold onto that feeling as I closed the door. Life might have moved on, but the stories, the laughter, and the bonds we'd built around them would always remain.

And who knows? We'll be closer to finding the Mochi Wala the next time we gather. Because some people, some stories, are just too important to let slip away.

The Quest

It had not even been a week since my friends and I met up when I received a call from one of my close friends, Viju. He sounded eager and a bit restless. “I just can’t get my mind off the Mochi Wala,” he said. “We need to find him.”

“I know what you mean,” I replied. “It’s been lingering in my mind since we last met. I want to discover what happened to him and where he is now.”

“Can we meet up soon?” Viju suggested. “We could start by looking for clues at the spot where he used to set up his cobbler stall. Maybe we could ask the landlord who rented the space to him.”

We exchanged ideas and plans for moving forward. We debated

whether to involve our other friends or take it up ourselves and inform them later, considering they might be busy with their own lives.

"Let's meet up this weekend," I proposed. "You can drive by my house and pick me up."

"Sounds like a plan," Viju agreed. "We'll get to the bottom of this."

With that, we ended the call, both of us feeling renewed purpose. The thought of the Mochi Wala and the mystery surrounding him had reignited our curiosity and determination. We were ready to embark on this new adventure, hoping to reconnect with a cherished part of our past.

Plans in motion - As the weekend approached, I grew more excited about the search. Memories of Mochi Wala's stories and his skilful work filled my mind. I wondered how he was doing and if he still remembered us.

On Saturday morning, Viju arrived at my house right on time. We greeted each other with a mix of anticipation and wistfulness. "Ready for this?" he asked, a grin spreading.

"Absolutely," I replied, climbing into his car. "Let's find our Mochi Wala."

We drove to the old neighbourhood, and the streets brought back memories.

We approached the spot where the Mochi Wala had his shop once. The current shopkeeper was

a middle-aged man who seemed friendly enough.

We introduced ourselves and explained our quest. “Do you remember the Mochi Wala who used to work here?” Viju asked.

The shopkeeper nodded. “I’m not aware if there was any Mochi Wala who rented this shop before me. But you can check with the landlord; maybe he’ll know something.”

“Where can I find the landlord?” asked Viju.

“You can find him at the gram panchayat office,” replied the shopkeeper. “He usually spends his time there with other folks.”

Village Emissary - As we drove deeper into the heart of the village, the familiar sights and sounds started to stir something in me. Passing the bustling night market again, fresh produce and spices aroma wafted through the air, tugging at childhood memories. I could almost hear my mum’s voice as we wandered through the stalls, her hands inspecting the freshest fruits and vegetables. At the same time, I trailed behind, clutching a paper cone of roasted peanuts.

“Remember when we used to run around that market as kids?” I said, turning to my friend in the passenger seat. “I’d get told off for knocking over baskets of mangoes.”

They chuckled. “And you still blame the mangoes for being in your way, right?”

“Obviously,” I replied with a grin.

Soon, we arrived at the gram panchayat office, nestled next to the old government school with its faded signboard and rusted swings in the yard. The sight was like stepping back in time.

Outside the office, a couple of elderly folks sat on a creaky wooden bench, their faces weathered and wise, etched with stories I could only imagine. They sat there as if time had slowed just for them, basking in the sun's warmth, their eyes half-closed in peaceful contentment.

One of them opened one eye lazily as we parked up, then closed it again as if to say, "Ah, just another visitor."

"This place hasn't changed a bit," I murmured, stepping out of the car. The air felt cleaner here, lighter somehow, free of the suffocating rush of city life.

The village seemed to exist in its own bubble of tranquillity. Unlike the city, where every moment feels like a race against time, the town ambled at its own pace. There was no urgency here, endless notifications or beeping alarms—just the soft murmur of life carrying on as it always had.

"Look at them," my friend whispered, gesturing to the elders. "They look like they've cracked the secret to life. Just soaking in the sun, not a care in the world."

"Maybe they have," I said, a hint of envy creeping into my voice.

Everything about this place felt in tune with the natural world. The villagers rose with the sun, their days dictated by the earth's rhythm. The men worked the fields, their tools glinting in the sunlight as they tilled the land. Women drew water from the well with practised ease, their laughter carrying across the open square as children played barefoot nearby, chasing each other with wild abandon.

Even the animals seemed at peace—cows lazily chewing cud,

goats wandering freely, and the occasional rooster crowing as if to remind everyone it was still his domain.

"What's that smell?" my friend asked, sniffing the air.

"Probably someone making rotis," I said, pointing to a nearby hut with smoke curling up from its chimney. "Or chai. Oh, how I'd kill for a proper village chai right now."

The pace of life here wasn't just slow—it was deliberate. Every moment seemed to matter, and every task was approached with care. The village would wind down naturally as the sun dipped below the horizon. There'd be no late-night scrolling, no artificial lights glaring into the darkness, just rest—pure, unhurried rest.

Standing there, taking it all in, I felt a deep connection to this place, its land and its people. There was a purity to their lives, a sense of contentment that was impossible to fake. They weren't chasing the next big thing, glued to screens or scrolling endlessly. They were living—in the moment, in harmony with the world around them.

"Do you ever feel like we've got it all backwards?" I asked, my voice barely above a whisper.

"How do you mean?"

"Like… everything we're chasing in the city—the money, the deadlines, the constant noise—it's not real. It's just layers of stress. But here…" I gestured around. "Here, they've got it right. They've got family, nature, and this sense of peace we always seek."

My friend nodded, their expression thoughtful. "It's humbling. Makes you realise happiness isn't about how much you have but how much you appreciate what you've got."

For a moment, neither of us spoke, both lost in our thoughts as we watched the village hum with quiet life.

Confrontation - We approached the older men, their serene chatter halting as we got closer. One of them, dressed in a crisp white kurta, dhoti, and a traditional turban, looked up slowly. His worn sandals gleamed in the sunlight, and he leaned heavily on a shabby wooden stick as if anchoring himself to the moment.

I cleared my throat, breaking the silence. "Excuse me, sir, we're looking for someone—the Mochi Wala. Do you remember him?"

The older man adjusted his grip on the stick and gave a faint nod, his eyes narrowing as if searching his memory. "The Mochi Wala," he began, his voice soft yet deliberate. "Yes, I remember him well. He was quite popular here—his shop was always buzzing, full of chatter and laughter."

He paused, his gaze distant now, lost in memories. "I was his landlord," he continued, his voice tinged with nostalgia. I rented him my shop. A good man, he was. He always paid his rent on time, not a day late. We'd sit together many evenings, drinking chai and swapping stories."

His expression grew sombre. "But one day, he was just… gone. The shop was locked, no sign of him. It was strange. No goodbye, no explanation. Just disappeared."

The man struggled to rise from the bench, leaning heavily on his stick. We stepped forward instinctively to help, but he waved us off.

He shuffled closer, squinting as if to see us more clearly.

"You might not remember us," I said, trying to jog his memory. "We were kids back then, always hanging around this area. The Mochi Wala used to tell us stories."

The man studied us for a moment before shaking his head. "No, I can't say I remember you," he admitted, "but I remember the Mochi Wala well. He loved children—his shop was always full of their laughter. He had a gift for making people happy."

Viju stepped in politely. "We'd like to find him, sir. He meant a lot to us growing up. Do you have any idea where he might be now?"

The landlord sighed, leaning heavily on his stick. "I liked him so much that I never renovated the shop after he left," he said, his tone reflective. "Kept it just as if he might walk back any day."

A flicker of hope appeared on his face. "I think he might have returned to his family," he said slowly. "They lived in another village not far from here. Bhavana, I believe it's called. You might want to ask some of the older folks around here. Someone's bound to know more."

We thanked him sincerely and were grateful for the lead. The man gave us a small smile before shuffling back to his bench, settling into his seat like he belonged there in the calmness of the moment.

"Good luck," he called as we turned to leave. "Tell him I still think of him if you find him."

As we walked away, the weight of the past seemed to lift slightly. There was a renewed sense of purpose among us. We'd been given a direction, and now it was up to us to follow it. The Mochi Wala wasn't just a memory anymore—he was a possibility waiting to be rediscovered.

As we strolled through the village streets, every corner seemed to whisper a memory; every breeze echoed our childhood laughter. The Mochi Wala's small shop had been a beacon for us back then. Rows of vibrant shoes neatly displayed, the comforting smell of freshly worked leather wafting through the air, and the man himself—spinning tales so vivid they made our small world feel impossibly vast.

"That shop was magic, wasn't it?" Viju mused, kicking at a stray pebble.

"Magic? It was like stepping into another dimension," I replied, grinning. "One minute, you were just a kid with scuffed sandals, and the next, you were a prince or a pirate or whatever his story turned you into."

We passed a fruit vendor who smiled knowingly, overhearing our chatter. "He was a gem, that Mochi Wala," she said suddenly. "Fixed my grandson's shoes once, wouldn't even take a rupee. I just asked the boy to listen to one of his stories. Said that was payment enough."

Another passerby, an older man smoking his beedi, joined in. "His laughter! I'll never forget it. Loud, hearty—like it came straight from his soul. You could hear it halfway across the village."

By the time we reached the Dhaba, we were parched and starving, the walk and the flood of emotions having taken their toll. The young waiter from before spotted us immediately, his face lighting up as if we were long-lost friends.

"You're back!" he exclaimed, hurrying to clean the table. "What brings you here again, sir?"

"Well," Viju began, collapsing into a chair, "firstly, we're starving. What's the fastest thing you can bring us?"

The waiter grinned mischievously, wiping his hands on his apron. "The fastest thing? I could bring you the bill right away!"

We burst out laughing, his cheeky humour catching us off guard. "All right, all right," I said, shaking my head. "But seriously, bring us something quick. And good!"

Minutes later, the waiter returned with a delicious Indian thali, its aroma tantalising. The sight of the neatly arranged dishes—a perfect blend of vibrant curries, fresh rotis, fragrant rice, and tangy pickles—made our mouths water.

"This is brilliant," one of us remarked mid-bite. "Who knew the village Dhaba had such a feast up its sleeve?"

The conversation naturally veered back to the Mochi Wala as we dug in. "We came back looking for him," I told the young waiter between bites.

The waiter paused thoughtfully. "There's someone you might want to meet," he said. "Tai—an old lady who lives nearby. She's been here forever and knows everyone's stories. She might know something about your Mochi Wala."

We finished our meal quickly, excitement bubbling over as the young waiter led us through narrow, winding lanes. The village seemed alive in a way we hadn't noticed earlier—children playing gully cricket, women chatting as they washed clothes by the well, and the occasional goat wandering.

“Are we close?” Viju asked, slightly out of breath.

“Nearly there,” the waiter replied, his voice calm as if he’d made this journey a thousand times. “Just around this corner.”

Finally, we stopped before a quaint, rustic cottage with a thatched roof and flowering vines creeping up its walls. The young waiter knocked gently on the wooden door, and we held our breath, hearts pounding with anticipation.

After a moment, the door creaked open, revealing a girl in her teens. She eyed us curiously, her expression polite but guarded. “Yes?” she asked, her tone clipped.

“We’re here to meet Tai,” the waiter explained, his voice tinged with respect.

The girl nodded but didn’t budge. “She’s resting. You’ll have to wait until she wakes up,” she said firmly before closing the door gently but decisively.

“Well, that was a bit of an anticlimax,” Viju muttered.

“Guess we’ll have to wait,” I said, resigned.

Back at the Dhaba, the waiter approached us again, his eyes sparkling with curiosity. “While you wait… could you tell me another story about the Mochi Wala?”

His request was like a balm to our frayed nerves. “All right,” I said, leaning back in my chair. “But this one’s a real classic. You’re in for a treat.”

The others perked up, too, their exhaustion momentarily forgotten. “This one better be good,” Viju teased.

“Oh, it’s not just good,” I smirked. “It’s legendary. It’s the one we begged him to tell over and over. The story of the Magical Umbrella.”

The waiter leaned in, elbows on the table, his face eager. “Magical Umbrella? What’s that about?”

“Ah,” I said, lowering my voice conspiratorially. “This wasn’t just any umbrella. It could make it rain in one place while keeping the person holding it completely dry. Perfect for a farmer who needed to water his crops or a cheeky kid who wanted to prank his friends.”

The group erupted into laughter, the waiter already hooked.

And so, I began weaving the tale, the Dhaba fading into the background as we were transported back to those magical evenings at the Mochi Wala’s shop. The words flowed effortlessly, and for a moment, it felt like we were kids again, wide-eyed and spellbound.

Even as we waited for Tai, it was clear: the Mochi Wala’s magic had never really left us. It was alive in the stories, laughter, and moments like this.

The Tone-Deaf Singer

In a quiet little town, there lived a cobbler named Umesh, a man known for his skill with leather and his calm, steady demeanour. His shop was a community cornerstone—shoes came in worn, battered, and left looking brand new. But as skilled as Umesh was with his craft, he had a rather unusual best mate: Raju, the self-proclaimed singer.

Raju loved music, but music didn't quite love him back. His voice had a… distinct quality, let's say—a cacophony of missed notes and strange melodies that made people laugh more than they applauded. Yet, Raju was blissfully unaware of his vocal shortcomings and proudly dubbed himself the "Songbird of the Town."

One evening, as the golden hues of sunset gave way to twilight, Umesh and Raju ambled down the cobbled streets after a long day. The town was settling into its peaceful nightly rhythm—shopkeepers shutting their stalls, the faint smell of dinner wafting through open windows, and an occasional stray dog trotting by. Raju suddenly stopped mid-stride, his face lighting up like a child with a new toy. "I've got the urge to sing!" he declared, his hands thrown dramatically into the air.

Umesh froze. This wasn't good. "No, no, Raju! Not now! The neighbourhood is resting. People don't want to hear your…

Uh, *unique* talent at this hour," he pleaded, eyes darting nervously to the darkened windows around them.

But Raju wasn't one to be dissuaded by a little thing like common sense. "Nonsense! A song is like a gift! And gifts should be shared!" With that, he cleared his throat and launched into what could generously be described as singing.

The first note—if you could call it that—rang out, slicing through the quiet night like a particularly unpleasant alarm clock. Umesh winced. Lights flickered in nearby houses, windows creaked open, and grumpy voices echoed through the street.

"Oi! Who's caterwauling at this hour?"

"Stop that racket, will you?"

"Some of us have to work in the morning!"

Before Umesh could stop him, a sandal flew out of a second-storey window, hitting Raju squarely on the shoulder.

"Oh!" Raju cried, clutching the spot. "How rude! Who throws a sandal at a singer?"

Umesh clutched his sides between trying to stop Raju and laughing at the absurdity. "Raju, stop singing before we get pelted with more than sandals!"

But Raju wasn't done. Oh no, the sandal was like fuel to his fire. "They don't understand art!" he bellowed before belting out a particularly jarring high note.

Another barrage of sandals, slippers, and a stray flip-flop rained down on them. Umesh tried to dodge, shielding himself with his bag. "Raju, you absolute lunatic! You're going to get us *both* killed!"

"Art is pain!" Raju shouted, dodging a particularly hefty slipper with surprising grace.

The neighbours, perhaps realising that their footwear arsenal was running low, eventually retreated. The street fell silent again, save for Raju, who was now humming softly, utterly unbothered by the chaos he'd caused.

Umesh looked at the pile of sandals littering the street, shaking his head. "You're unbelievable," he muttered, though he couldn't suppress a grin.

Raju bent down and picked up an adorable leather sandal, holding it to the moonlight. "Well, at least I've got a new pair of shoes out of this," he winked.

Umesh burst out laughing, slapping Raju on the back. "You're mad, you know that? Completely mad."

As they continued their walk home, Umesh couldn't help but smile. Life with Raju was chaotic, sure, but it was never dull. And as Raju hummed softly to himself, undoubtedly plotting his next "performance," Umesh braced himself for whatever adventure—or disaster—might come next.

Raju would sing on the roads, at functions, and even at weddings. But wherever he sang, people would cover their ears and throw slippers and sandals at him. The poor singer would leave with a pile of footwear, feeling dejected.

One day, Umesh saw an opportunity in this. He'd collect the thrown shoes and sandals and bring them to his shop. He would mend and refurbish them, then display them at a lower price in his shop for sale. The sale board outside his shop would say,

"Second Hand and Refurbish Footwear for sale"

His shop soon became famous for its "Singer's Specials" section, where people could buy slippers and sandals at a discount. The cobbler would joke, "Raju's singing may not be melodious, but it brings music to my shop!"

As Raju continued to sing (despite the protests), Umesh's business flourished. People would come from all over to hear the "worst singer in town" and see what new additions Umesh had in his shop. The once quiet cobbler's shop was now bustling with customers, all eager to get their hands on the unique "Singer's Specials."

Though often disheartened by the reactions to his singing, Raju found solace in his friend Umesh, who benefitted from it. He continued to sing with all his heart, knowing that each off-key note was helping his friend's business thrive.

It was a fine morning that promised nothing but good things. Umesh had a plan—he needed to visit the neighbouring village to stock up on raw leather goods for his shop. His usual supplier had promised a good deal, and Umesh knew saving a bit here and there would go a long way. But this time, he decided to take Raju along.

"Raju," Umesh said as they set off, the sun just beginning to paint the sky in shades of gold, "you've been cooped up too long with your singing woes. A bit of fresh air and mountain scenery will do you good. Who knows? Maybe it'll even inspire you to sing in tune!"

Raju rolled his eyes but couldn't hide his grin. "Oi, don't push your luck, mate. My voice is unique, not bad."

The journey was breathtaking. They passed lush green fields where cows grazed lazily, sparkling rivers meandering through the landscape, and majestic mountains towering majestically in the distance. Raju, who'd been a bit sulky, started to loosen up.

"Look at those mountains, Umesh!" he said, his face lighting up. "They're magnificent! Makes you feel tiny, doesn't it?"

Umesh chuckled, glad to see his friend perking up. "Yep. Sometimes, all it takes is a change of scenery to remind us there's more to life than our problems."

When they finally arrived at the bustling market, the place was alive with energy. Vendors shouted out their wares, from fresh produce to handmade trinkets, and the air was filled with the tantalising aroma of street food.

"You crack on with your leather business," Raju said, already eyeing the stalls. "I'll have a little wander."

"Just don't get into any trouble," Umesh warned, though he knew it was a futile request.

Raju waved him off and began exploring, his curiosity leading him from one colourful stall to the next. Then, like a moth drawn to a flame, his eyes locked onto something extraordinary—a colossal bell tower standing tall in the heart of the village.

"Now that's a proper bell," he muttered, feeling an irresistible urge to investigate.

Without a second thought, he bolted up the tower's winding stairs, his excitement building with each step. Reaching the top, he spotted the massive rope attached to the bell. "Let's see what this beauty sounds like," he said, gripping the rope tightly.

And then, with all the strength he could muster, Raju yanked it.

BONGGGGG!!!

The sound was deafening, reverberating through the valley like an apocalyptic alarm. Villagers froze in their tracks; their faces lifted towards the bell tower in shock. For a moment, it was as if the world had stopped turning.

Umesh felt his stomach drop when he was haggling over leather prices. "Oh no… no, no, no! He didn't…"But he knew. He knew. The villagers quickly snapped out of their stupor, their expressions shifting from confusion to annoyance to fear. The bell wasn't just a bell—it was a warning signal. For generations, it had alerted the village of imminent danger—bandits, fires, or worse.

Murmurs of “What’s happening?” and “Who rang the bell?” rippled through the crowd.

Blissfully unaware of the chaos he’d caused, Raju stood at the top of the tower, grinning like a kid who’d just discovered a new toy.

“Oi! You up there!” an elderly villager shouted, shaking his fist. “What do you think you’re doing, ringing that bell? Are you trying to give us all a heart attack?

“Panting from sprinting to the tower, Umesh arrived just in time to see the commotion unfold. He tilted his head back, squinting at

Raju, who was waving cheerily.

“Raju! Get down here, you idiot!” Umesh bellowed, half in fury, half in exasperation.

Raju descended slowly, the grin never leaving his face. “Blimey, Umesh, that bell’s got some lungs on it! Did you hear how far the sound carried?”

Umesh grabbed him by the arm as soon as he was within reach. “You absolute muppet! Do you realise you’ve just triggered the village alarm? They think we’re under attack!”

The villagers, now gathering in a heated mob, looked anything but amused. Umesh turned to them, his hands raised in apology.

“I’m so sorry!” he said earnestly. “It was a mistake—my friend here is… well, let’s just say he’s *enthusiastic* and didn’t realise the bell’s significance.”

"Enthusiastic?" a burly man growled. "He scared the life out of my missus! We thought it was an invasion!"

The villagers were unforgiving, their anger bubbling to the surface like water on the boil. "He must be punished," one declared, his voice firm and unwavering. Others nodded in agreement, their faces grim. "Raju will spend the night alone and unprotected, out in the open, to face the evil spirits that roam our lands," another added as if the punishment was as inevitable as the setting sun.

The crowd murmured approval, and the decision was final. The villagers retreated to their homes, bolting their doors and lighting oil lamps to ward off the looming darkness. The mood in the air shifted from anger to uneasy anticipation. The village seemed to hold its breath, waiting to see what would happen to Raju.

Raju stood in the village square, his heart sinking as the reality of his situation hit him. "Alone?" he muttered to himself. "Evil spirits?" His knees felt weak, and he glanced around helplessly.

"Not alone," came Umesh's voice, steady and reassuring. He stepped forward, placing a hand on Raju's trembling shoulder. "You think I'm leaving you to face this lot alone? Forget it. We'll deal with whatever comes—together."

Raju's eyes filled with gratitude. "You'd do that for me?"

"Well," Umesh teased, "it's either that or listen to you belt out songs about your doom for the next week. Might as well get it over with."

The two settled under the old tower bell, its shadow looming large against the flickering lamplight. The silence was deafening, broken only by the occasional chirp of a cricket or the whisper of wind through the trees.

Raju fidgeted nervously, his eyes darting to every shadow. “Umesh, what if the spirits are real?” he whispered.

“Then they’ll be real sorry they picked a fight with us,” Umesh quipped, leaning back against the bell’s frame.

“But what if—”

“Raju,” Umesh interrupted, raising an eyebrow. “Stop overthinking. If anything shows up, we’ll handle it. And if nothing shows up, we’ll laugh about this tomorrow.”

As the hours dragged on, the oppressive silence grew heavier. Raju began to shiver, more from fear than the cold. “I can’t take it anymore,” he said, standing up abruptly. “It’s too quiet. Too creepy.”

“What are you doing?” Umesh asked, his tone wary.

“I’m going to sing,” Raju declared, his chest puffed out with resolve. “If we’re going down, we’re going down to music.”

Umesh groaned. “Oh, for the love of— Fine. Sing. But keep it below glass-shattering levels, yeah?”

Raju ignored him, launching into an enthusiastic, wildly off-key rendition of a local folk tune. His voice echoed through the empty square, startling birds from their roosts and probably scaring a few nearby dogs.

As Raju’s “singing” continued, the wind began to pick up. A

chill crept into the air, and the lamplight flickered ominously. Umesh straightened, his teasing expression replaced by one of caution. "Raju… maybe tone it down a bit."

"Why?" Raju asked, oblivious. "I'm just getting to the chorus."

Before Umesh could answer, a dark shadow swooped across the square. Both men froze, their eyes widening as more shapes began circling overhead.

"Spirits?" Raju squeaked, his voice rising an octave.

Umesh nodded grimly. "Looks like it."

The dark forms drew closer, their eerie hum growing louder. Raju's grip on Umesh's arm tightened. "What do we do?"

Umesh's eyes darted around, searching for inspiration. "Sing louder," he finally said.

"Are you serious?" Raju asked, incredulous.

"Deadly serious. If your singing can scare off half the village, it'll work on them, too.

With nothing to lose, Raju drew a deep breath and let loose the loudest, most off-key note he could muster. The sound reverberated through the square like a banshee's wail. The spirits faltered mid-flight, their circling disrupted as if confused.

"Keep going!" Umesh shouted, his voice barely audible over Raju's cacophony.

Emboldened, Raju launched into another verse, each note more ear-splitting than the last. The spirits recoiled, their forms shimmering as they scattered into the night.

The villagers peeked out from behind the curtains in their homes, their jaws dropping at the sight. “Is he… scaring them off?” one whispered.

“It’s a miracle,” another murmured, though their expression suggested they weren’t sure whether to laugh or cry.

As the last spirit fled, Raju finally stopped, gasping for air. Umesh clapped him on the back, grinning. “I can’t believe it. Your singing saved us.”

Raju, still catching his breath, managed a sheepish smile. “Told you I had talent.”

As the sun rose the following day, its golden rays spilling over the mountains and fields, a peculiar scene awaited the villagers. They had anticipated terror and chaos but found something entirely unexpected. Raju and Umesh, huddled under the tower bell, were fast asleep, looking surprisingly peaceful.

The villagers approached cautiously, bearing gifts of fresh fruits, warm cakes, and intricate ornaments. Their anger from the previous night had melted into admiration. The duo’s unexpected bravery—and Raju’s off-key singing that had seemingly driven away the spirits—had won them over.

“Wake up, heroes!” an elderly villager called out, his voice tinged with newfound respect. The commotion stirred Umesh, who rubbed his eyes groggily. At the same time, Raju yawned and stretched, blinking in confusion at the crowd gathered around them.

"What's going on?" Raju mumbled, still half-asleep.

"You've saved the village," the elder announced. "We owe you our gratitude."

The day quickly turned into a celebration. Raju and Umesh were treated like royalty. Freshly prepared meals were served, and the head of the village presented them with the prestigious key to the town—a symbol of their honorary status.

"You're welcome to stay here as long as you like," the elder said warmly. "This is your home now."

Raju's chest swelled with pride while Umesh tried to suppress a grin. "Well, that's unexpected," Umesh murmured. "We went from troublemakers to heroes overnight."

News of their bravery spread like wildfire, reaching neighbouring villages. Curious visitors flocked to see the duo. Umesh's leatherwork became the talk of the town, and people lined up to buy his shoes. Some even donated their old, worn-out footwear, which Umesh repaired and sold as second-hand treasures. His shop bustled with activity, the air filled with the rhythmic tapping of tools and the hum of happy customers.

Raju, meanwhile, discovered an unexpected fan base. Villagers gifted him musical instruments and encouraged him to sing. Requests poured in for him to perform—not just entertain but supposedly drive away evil spirits. "The tone-deaf hero," they called him affectionately, though the irony wasn't lost on him.

But not everyone was thrilled by their success. The village priests, once the go-to figures for spiritual matters, found their influence waning. People no longer sought their help, turning instead to the unlikely duo. Resentment brewed, and the priests hatched a plan to reclaim their power.

Late one night, the priests gathered in a clearing deep in the forest under the eerie light of a full moon. Their chants echoed through the trees as they summoned the malevolent spirits of "Kaalakoota" and cast spells designed to silence Raju's voice and unravel Umesh's fortune.

In the village, however, an invisible "Raksha Kavach"—a protective aura born of the villagers' love and admiration—shielded Raju and Umesh. The priests' spells fizzled out, leaving them frustrated and desperate.

Failing at sorcery, the priests turned to manipulation. They whispered deceitful words into Umesh's ear. "Raju is overshadowing you," they said. "You're the real talent. His fame is holding you back."

To Raju, they murmured, "Umesh is riding on your success. You're the true star. He's just a cobbler."

But the bond between Umesh and Raju was unshakable. They laughed off the priests' attempts to sow discord. "Do they think we'd fall for that?" Raju chuckled. "Mate, you're the best cobbler around. I'd be barefoot without you."

"And you're the most entertaining singer I know," Umesh replied with a grin. "Not many can say they've scared away spirits with their voice."

Realising they couldn't break the duo, the priests left the village in defeat, seeking new territories to regain their influence.

Life continued to flourish for Umesh and Raju. Umesh's shop expanded, and he began teaching apprentices the art of shoemaking. Raju's performances became legendary, his off-key singing a source of joy and laughter for all.

Their friendship remained the cornerstone of their success. Together, they were unstoppable—a testament to the power of camaraderie and resilience. And that's the end of this whimsical story that I remember as told to us by our beloved Mochi Wala.

As the young waiter cleared our plates, he piped up, "I think I've got a voice like Raju's. Maybe I can scare away spirits, too!"

We burst into laughter. "Don't quit your day job just yet," Viju teased, winking at him.

"I'm more of a bathroom singer myself," Viju added with a cheeky grin. "But every time I sing, I'll think of Raju and his heroic wailing."

We all laughed, the story of Umesh and Raju lingering in the air like a warm embrace. It was a reminder of simpler times, friendships forged in laughter and adventure.

Moral of the Story - The tale of "The Cobbler and the Tone-Deaf Singer" teaches us that true strength lies in unity, kindness, and embracing our unique qualities. We can overcome challenges and find joy in the most unexpected places.

Unfolding the Past

As we exchanged pleasantries, the same young girl approached us, her eyes sparkling excitedly. "My grand-aunt has woken up," she said, "you may speak with her if you please." Her words were like a gentle nudge, bringing us back to the purpose of our visit. We exchanged curious glances, wondering what wisdom or stories the older woman might share with us.

The young girl led us inside the simple yet well-maintained house, with decent decor that reflected a warm and welcoming atmosphere. With her wrinkled face and gloomy eyes, the old lady slowly got up from her bed, trying to recognise us as if searching for familiar faces from her past.

We sat beside her on the chairs offered to us, and I explained our visit. "We grew up in this neighbourhood as kids and spent countless hours in Mochi Wala's shop, especially during rainy seasons, listening to his captivating fairy tales and folk stories."

Viju added, "We wanted to meet him and wish him good health. "The old lady's face softened, and she grinned, lost in thought as if transported back to a bygone era.

"You've brought back my unforgettable memories, memories that had been tucked away in the recesses of my mind, memories that I thought had faded with time, but now, with your visit, they come flooding back like a gentle rain reviving a parched landscape, bringing with them the sweet scent of longing and the warmth of a bygone era."

Unfolding the past -The old lady's eyes sparkled with rumination as she remembered Mochi Wala's early days. "I still remember it like it was yesterday," she said, her voice filled with a warm, fuzzy tone.

"A young man, full of ambition and vitality, setting up his shop with so much enthusiasm. He carried all his belongings on his bicycle, making multiple trips from home to the shop, refusing help or support from anyone. His determination and self-reliance left a lasting impression on me."

She paused, lost in thought, before continuing, "After setting up his shop, he installed an altar and pictures of saints and deities, offering prayers with devotion. He sat, looking lively and hopeful, waiting for his first customer. I was that customer, and I must admit, I entered his shop, pretending to need my sandals mended. I was very impressed by his simplicity and kindness. He welcomed me with a warm smile, offering me a seat on the long bench, and I felt at ease in his presence."

A sly smile spread across her face as she confessed, "From that day on, I found every excuse to visit his shop - buying, mending, or even deliberately breaking my shoes and sandals just to catch a glimpse of him. I had a secret crush on him, and he knew it too. He would eagerly await my visits, his eyes lighting up with excitement whenever I entered his shop with a new excuse. It was a game we played, and I cherished every moment."

Our clandestine meetings became a regular affair as the days turned into weeks. His cobbler shop remained our secret rendezvous. I would watch in wonder as he worked his magic with leather, crafting shoes and sandals with precision and care.

Time stood still as I observed his skilled hands, mesmerised by how he brought raw materials to life. The sound of hammering, the smell of leather, and the sight of his focused expression all blended to create an unforgettable experience. And with each passing day, my admiration for him grew, as did our unspoken connection.

The old lady's eyes overflowed with tears as she recounted the heart-wrenching tale of her lost love, Mochi Wala. "I was torn away from him suddenly, without even a chance to bid him farewell," she sobbed, her voice trembling like a leaf. "Family emergency was what my family told me it was; days turned into months, and the ache in my heart only intensified, a constant reminder that I had left a part of myself behind."

Meanwhile, Mochi Wala was consumed by despair, wondering why the young girl had vanished. He thought she had abandoned him, and his heart shattered into a million pieces. Dejected and defeated, he left everything behind, including his beloved shop, symbolising their love. He roamed from village to village, searching for her, but fate was cruel, and she was nowhere to be found.

The weight of his sorrow was crushing, and he couldn't bear the thought of returning to their village, where every memory would torment him. So, he settled in a nearby town, hoping to escape the haunting memories and find solace in a new beginning. Yet, his heart remained forever tied to hers, a prisoner of their love.

Years passed, and she returned, driven by a fierce determination to find her lost love. She rented a house near his old shop, waiting patiently for his return, her heart beating with hope and trepidation.

But when she finally found him, her world came crashing down. He was playing with a couple of children, and she assumed he had moved on, that their love was a distant memory. Little did she know, the children were his brothers, and he had never married, his heart still belonging to her alone.

As she uttered these words, tears began to roll down her eyes like a river, unstoppable and unrelenting. The room fell silent as if the weight of her emotions had sucked the air out of it. I glanced at Viju, and he met my gaze, frozen in a moment of empathetic understanding. The young girl beside her looked on, confusion etched on her face, unsure how to process the moment's intensity. We had unwittingly touched a deep well of grief, and the old lady's defences began to crumble. She seemed to be holding her breath, waiting for permission to release the emotions she had bottled up for so long. And then, like a dam breaking, she burst into tears, her body shaking with sobs.

Homecoming

We tried to console her, offering comfort and support, but she was beyond solace. We asked her if she could take us to Mochi Wala, but she hesitated, unsure if she was ready to confront the past. Perhaps she feared that seeing him again would stir up emotions she had long suppressed, or she thought it was better to leave things as they were, sparing him the guilt of knowing she had waited for him all these years.

But we insisted, explaining that it was essential for us to meet him, to understand the depth of their love and the tragedy that had befallen them. Finally, she relented, agreeing to take us to him, though her eyes betrayed deep trepidation.

We embarked on our journey the same day, eager to reunite the star-crossed lovers. Our car was filled with emotions - excitement, sadness, and anticipation. The old lady, accompanied by her grandniece, sat beside us, her eyes fixed on the road ahead, her hands clasped together in a mix of anxiety and hope.

We couldn't help but think about the man who had brought so much joy to our childhood yet had suffered a heart-wrenching love story. Our hearts ached with empathy, and we were determined to connect him with his lost love, to bring closure to their unfinished tale.

The scenery outside changed as we drove, but our thoughts remained fixed on the couple. We imagined their young love, secret meetings, and future dreams together. We thought about the pain of their separation, the years of longing, and the what-ifs that had haunted them. Our determination grew with each passing mile, and we knew we had to make this reunion happen.

The six-hour drive felt like an eternity; our fingers crossed in anticipation. We prayed that he had waited for her all these years, that he was still single, and that their love could be rekindled. We hoped the spark that had once burned so brightly between them still flickered, waiting to be fanned into a flame again.

As we entered the village, our hearts sank with emotions - gloom, hope, and uncertainty. We hoped that Mochi Wala still lived there, that he hadn't moved away, and that we would find him in the same place where their love story had begun. The village seemed quiet as if waiting for us, and we knew our arrival would change their lives forever.

We took a deep breath, preparing ourselves for what lay ahead, and drove towards the destination that would reunite the lovers.

We finally reached the house, but our excitement was short-lived. The house seemed deserted, and our hearts sank with disappointment. We had waited so long, driven for hours, and now it seemed our efforts might be in vain. We stood there, defeated, wondering if we had made a mistake.

Much-awaited climax - Suddenly, a group of children burst out of the house, laughing and playing, and our dear Mochi Wala emerged, chasing after them. Time stood still as we gazed at him, our minds flashing back to our childhood memories. He looked older, his hair grey, but his eyes still twinkled with the same warmth and kindness we remembered. His smile, though worn, still had the same infectious charm.

Viju and I exchanged a glance, both of us transported back to a time when life was simpler and Mochi Wala's stories had filled our afternoons with wonder. We couldn't believe our eyes - the man who had been etched in our memories for so long was standing right before us.

Mochi Wala noticed our car parked outside and that we were getting out of it. He slowed down, his eyes narrowing slightly as he tried to place us. And then, as recognition dawned on him, his face lit up with surprise and curiosity.

He walked towards us, his gait a little slower than we remembered, but his warmth and hospitality radiated from him like a beacon.

As we approached him, his eyes locked onto the old lady, and time stood still. They stared at each other, tears streaming down their faces like rivers, the air thick with unspoken emotions. The silence was deafening, a heavy blanket that wrapped around their souls.

Finally, she broke the silence, asking about his life in a voice barely above a whisper. He replied, trembling, "I never married." As if he knew what she was about to ask him.

The old lady's face crumpled, and she sobbed uncontrollably, her body shaking like a leaf. "I'm so sorry I left without a word," she said, her voice cracking. "I waited for you, but my family wouldn't let me return. I've spent my entire life waiting for you, hoping you'd return for me."

Mochi Wala's face contorted in anguish, and he embraced her tightly. "I've waited for you too, my dearest," he whispered, his voice trembling. "I never stopped loving you."

As they held each other, the years melted away, and they were transported back to their secret rendezvous, surrounded by the sweet scent of leather and the gentle hammering of his tools.

Their love, once thought lost, had endured a flame that burned bright and true.

At that moment, we knew their love story was far from over. It was a testament to the power of true love, which can transcend time, distance, and circumstances. As we watched them reunite, our hearts swelled with joy, knowing that Mochi Wala and his lady had finally found their happily ever after.

As I watched the Mochi Wala and his companion together, a wave of regret washed over me, and tears began to roll down my eyes. I couldn't help but think about the what-ifs. "Oh, why did I not try to return to the village sooner?" I thought to myself, my mind racing with the possibilities. "If only I had returned earlier, I could have reunited them years ago. I could have saved them from all those years of longing and heartache."

I thought about the Mochi Wala, living his life without the love of his life by his side, and the old lady, carrying the weight of her memories, her heart heavy with the thought of what could have been. I imagined the countless moments they had missed together, the laughter they had never shared, the adventures they had never had.

"If only I had acted sooner," I thought, "maybe they would have been together much earlier in life, enjoying each other's company, growing old together. Perhaps they would have had children, grandchildren, and a lifetime of memories to cherish. "The thought of all that lost time was almost too much to bear.

I felt a pang of guilt for not trying harder to find the Mochi Wala and for not making more of an effort to reconnect with him sooner. But as I looked at the two of them, finally together, I knew that we had played a small part in bringing them back to each other. And as I wiped away my tears, I smiled, knowing that sometimes, even the most minor actions can lead to the greatest joys.

As we sat there, surrounded by the gentle rustle of leaves and the warm glow of the setting sun, the young girl snuggled up beside us, her eyes fixed on the Mochi Wala and his companion. We watched, mesmerised, as they tried to catch up on a lifetime of moments, their faces aglow with happiness.

The air was filled with the sweet scent of blooming flowers and the soft chirping of birds, creating a sense of serenity that wrapped around us like a warm blanket.

Time lost all meaning as we sat there, minutes melting into hours, but we didn't notice. We were too caught up in the moment's joy, too grateful to be a part of this reunion. Seeing the Mochi Wala and his companion together, holding hands and laughing, was the most precious gift we could ever give him back for all the stories he had shared with us, all the laughter he had brought into our lives, and all the joy he had given us.

As the hours passed, the sky transformed into a kaleidoscope of colours, a breathtaking sunset that seemed to match the moment's beauty. We didn't want it to end; we didn't want to break the spell that had been cast. But as the stars began to twinkle in the night sky, we knew this was just the beginning of a new chapter in the Mochi Wala's life, one that we were honoured to have played a part in.

As the last rays of daylight faded, the evening sky transformed into a mesmerising canvas of soft pinks, blues, and purples, a breathtaking sunset that seemed to linger forever. But as the stars began to twinkle, the moon, now a silver crescent in the sky, cast its gentle light upon us, bathing the scene in an ethereal glow. The world seemed to slow down as if nature favoured this reunion's beauty.

Then, the Mochi Wala and the old lady approached us, their faces radiant with happiness and joy. Their eyes sparkled like the stars above, their smiles as wide as the moon. They walked hand in hand, their steps slow and deliberate, as if they were savouring every moment of this newfound love.

As they drew closer, the warmth of their presence enveloped us, filling our hearts with a sense of contentment and peace. We could see the deep connection between them, the love that had endured despite the passing of time, and it filled us with a sense of wonder and awe. They seemed to be basking in the joy of each other's company, their happiness infectious, spreading to all of us around them.

The Mochi Wala's eyes, still shining with happiness, turned to us, and he smiled warmly. "I'm so sorry; I got too emotional and forgot about you two," he said, his voice filled with genuine apology. "Please, forgive an old man's sentimental heart."

Viju, with a gentle smile, asked, "Do you recognise us?" His voice was soft and understanding, knowing that the Mochi Wala's memories might be hazy.

The Mochi Wala's face scrunched up in concentration, his eyes searching our faces, trying to recall the memories. He looked at us with a tinge of guilt, embarrassed that he couldn't place us. But then, I helped him out, my voice filled with longing.

"We are those kids who used to spend time in your shop, and you used to tell us all the folk tales and fairy tales," I said, a smile spreading across my face.

As the Mochi Wala's face lit up with recognition, he exclaimed, "Ah, those mischievous kids who would gather around me every evening, eyes wide with wonder!" He chuckled, remembering the countless stories he had spun for them. Viju and I smiled, feeling like we were transported back to our childhood, surrounded by the sweet scent of mochi and the magic of the Mochi Wala's tales.

The old lady, noticing our reunion, joined in, her eyes sparkling with curiosity. "Tell me, what brings you two back to our village after all these years?" she asked, her voice warm and gentle. We took turns sharing our story, explaining how we had never forgotten the Mochi Wala's stories and their impact on our lives.

As we spoke, the Mochi Wala's eyes grew misty, and he reached out, placing a hand on each of our shoulders.

"I'm so proud of the people you've become," he said, his voice trembling with emotion. "I always knew my stories would stay with you kids, but I never imagined they would bring you back to me all these years later." The five of us sat there, surrounded by the quiet of the evening, the only sound the soft chirping of crickets and the occasional barking of dogs in the distance.

All he could remember was a few young children whom he used to entertain with his made-up fairy tales and folk stories. He loved kids, and he loved to tell them stories; it made him feel like a child himself, full of wonder and imagination. The Mochi Wala's eyes twinkled, and he said, "I'm so glad you're here! You've brought back so many fond memories!"

As the night wore on, we sat around the bonfire, mesmerised by the flickering flames that danced across the faces of our companions. The open-air, lush green meadows and tall trees surrounding us allowed a calm wind to blow, making the nights more remarkable in the village. The atmosphere was serene, with the only sounds being the occasional crackle of the fire and the distant hooting of owls.

The Mochi Wala was engrossed in conversation with the old

lady, their faces aglow with warmth and nostalgia. We didn't want to interrupt their moment, but our eagerness to hear a story from the Mochi Wala after many years was intense. It was as if we had been waiting for an eternity, our anticipation building with each passing moment.

I finally broke the silence, my voice barely containing my excitement. "Sir, would you mind telling us a story, something we haven't heard before?" I asked, my eyes locked on the Mochi Wala's, hoping against hope that he would agree.

The Mochi Wala looked at us, his eyes twinkling with a hint of mischief. "I have just the one," he said, his voice low. "A story I've been saving for a long time."

We were thrilled, our faces lighting up with anticipation. We were all ears, attentive, and completely absorbed in the moment. The cold weather was forgotten, and the warmth of our excitement replaced the chill in the air. We could only think about what was coming next from the Mochi Wala's lips. The world around us melted away, leaving only the promise of a captivating tale waiting to be spun by the master storyteller himself. The Mochi Wala paused, collecting his thoughts, as the flames danced and crackled, casting a hypnotic spell on us. "Where do I begin?" he mused, his eyes gazing into the fire as if searching for the right words. "Well, it's going to be a short one," he added, a hint of a smile on his lips.

We remained silent, our eyes fixed on him, our minds racing with anticipation. We didn't care if the story was short or long; all we wanted was to be transported to a world of wonder, to be captivated by Mochi Wala's words. The length of the story was irrelevant; it was the tale itself that mattered.In that moment, time stood still. The world around us melted away, leaving only the Mochi Wala, the fire, and us, his eager listeners. The air was thick with expectation, and we were on the edge of our seats, our hearts pounding in unison, waiting for the story to begin.

And then, with a gentle nod, the Mochi Wala started to speak, his voice intertwining a spell that would take us over time;

Cobbler and The Blacksmith

In the kingdom of Maheshwar, two artisans served King Mahesh and his court: Piyush, the cobbler, and Jayam, the blacksmith. Each played a pivotal role in maintaining the kingdom's glory, yet their paths were as different as night and day. Piyush, humble and kind, served with love, while Jayam, consumed by pride, viewed his craft as a means of asserting dominance.

Piyush's small shop stood near the palace walls, open to all who sought his skill. The shop had no doors—just a blanket shielding it from the elements—and an inviting air of simplicity. People came not only for repairs but also for his warmth. His mantra was simple: "Serve with love." Piyush repaired the shoes of soldiers, ministers, and even ordinary folk without expecting payment if they couldn't afford it. His work, infused with compassion, stitched not just soles but hearts.

In contrast, Jayam's forge near the palace gates radiated arrogance. The clang of steel resonated as a testament to his self-importance. Jayam revelled in his reputation as the kingdom's premier blacksmith. He charged exorbitant fees, delayed orders, and basked in the power of being indispensable. His weapons gleamed as sharply as his pride, yet his craft lacked the humanity that Piyush brought to his work.

One day, as Piyush repaired a soldier's boots, he overheard whispers of unrest. The neighbouring kingdom of Malakai was threatening war, and its ambitious King was eager to expand his domain. Soldiers spoke of sleepless nights and the looming spectre of battle.

"We need strong armour," one soldier remarked to another. "Jayam's steel is unmatched, but his delays cost us precious time."

Piyush's hands paused for a moment, his thoughts heavy. While Jayam's steel was strong, its clanging betrayed the soldiers' positions, a dangerous flaw in the face of stealthy enemies. An idea began to form in his mind, but he said nothing, quietly finishing the soldier's boots.

Meanwhile, Jayam's greed blinded him to the urgency of the kingdom's plight. Soldiers who came to him were met with demands for higher payments and dismissive instructions to return later. One such soldier, dejected and desperate, confided in Piyush.

"Jayam's arrogance will cost us the war," he said, his voice trembling with frustration. "We need someone who truly serves the kingdom."

Piyush's resolve hardened. "I may not forge steel, but I'll do what I can to help," he replied, his heart swelling with purpose.

Amid rising tensions, King Mahesh had a peculiar dream. A mystic voice whispered to him, "The path to victory lies not in steel but in silence." The cryptic message unsettled the King, who summoned his advisors and priests to decipher it.

The royal announcer spread the word across the kingdom: "Hear ye, hear ye! The King seeks wisdom! Whoever can decipher the meaning of these words shall be rewarded!"

The announcement reached Piyush as he worked in the market square. He paused, the words resonating deeply. "Silence," he murmured, his mind racing. Could it mean…?

Meanwhile, Jayam dismissed the announcement with a scoff. "Steel wins wars, not riddles," he declared, his apprentices nodding in agreement.

That evening, Piyush presented himself at the palace gates, requesting an audience with the King. The guards hesitated, but his earnestness won them over. Guided into the grand hall, Piyush bowed deeply before King Mahesh.

"Your Majesty," he began, his voice steady, "I believe I understand the message. Steel may protect, but it betrays. Silence is the key to stealth. Let me craft light, silent, and efficient leather armour and horseshoes to aid our soldiers in moving like shadows."

The King's eyes widened with interest. "Leather armour? Silent horseshoes? This is a bold idea, cobbler."

Jayam, who had been listening, burst into the room, his face red with fury. "Leather armour? Preposterous!" he bellowed. "My steel has protected this kingdom for years! This cobbler's flimsy leather will crumble in battle!"

Piyush stood firm. "With respect, Your Majesty, steel clinks and clanks, giving away our soldiers' positions. Leather whispers, allowing them to strike unseen. Let me prove my worth."

The King's gaze shifted between the two artisans. Finally, he nodded. "Piyush, you have my trust. Begin your work immediately."

As Piyush laboured tirelessly, Jayam's jealousy simmered into sabotage. Under darkness, he tampered with Piyush's supplies, slashing leather and misaligning tools. The next morning, Piyush discovered the damage. His heart sank, but his resolve remained unbroken.

Working through the night, he repaired the ruined pieces, his hands steady despite the exhaustion. He fashioned lightweight armour, silent horseshoes, and helmets with leather castings, ensuring each piece was flawless.

When the soldiers donned the leather gear, they marvelled at its flexibility and silence. Even the horses moved without a sound, their hoofbeats muffled by Piyush's craftsmanship.

The King's men, equipped with Piyush's creations, embarked on a daring mission to infiltrate the enemy camp. The soldiers moved like shadows, undetected, until it was too late for King Malakai's forces. The silent armour proved its worth, and the kingdom of Maheshwar emerged victorious.

When the soldiers returned, King Mahesh greeted them at the palace gates. "Victory is ours," he declared, his voice filled with pride. "And thanks to Piyush, whose wisdom and craft have saved us all."

The King summoned both artisans to the throne room. Turning to Piyush, he said, "Your innovation has secured our kingdom's future. From this day forward, you shall be the Royal Cobbler, serving the palace exclusively."

Then, addressing Jayam, his tone hardened. "Your arrogance and sabotage endangered our soldiers and our kingdom. I have no place for such treachery. You are dismissed from palace service."

Jayam's face fell, and his pride shattered. He left the palace, his footsteps heavy with regret.

Piyush, humbled by the honour, bowed low. "I serve not for reward but for the joy of serving," he said, echoing through the hall.

Piyush's name became a legend; his story was passed down through generations. His humility and innovation reminded the kingdom that true strength lay not in pride but in love and resilience.

Moral of the Story - "And that," the Mochi Wala said, concluding his tale, "is the story of Piyush, the humble cobbler who changed the fate of a kingdom. His humility and determination proved that greatness doesn't require grand gestures; sometimes, the quiet strength of a kind heart can move mountains and shape destinies."

Viju clapped enthusiastically. "I had goosebumps just listening to you! Your storytelling magic hasn't faded one bit."

The group chuckled, the warmth of shared memories filling the air.

The young girl listening nearby piped up, "Can you teach me to tell stories like that?"

The Mochi Wala smiled, his eyes twinkling. "Of course, my dear. Stories are meant to be shared."

And so, under the moonlit sky, a new chapter began. The Mochi Wala, the old lady, and the young girl started a new journey together, filled with stories, laughter, and the sweet taste of mochi. The village, once filled with sorrow, now echoed with joy and hope, all thanks to the power of love and the magic of stories.

The adventure of a lifetime deserves an audience! I'm itching to share our incredible journey with the old gang and relive the memories we thought were lost in time.

"As we reunite with the Mochi Wala, I hope he'll be delighted to see us, his old friends, still young at heart. We may have grown up, but our love for wonder and magic remains unchanged. We would love to gather around him again and let the enchantment of his folk tales and fairy stories transport us back to a world of childhood marvels. We are forever children in his presence, with hearts full of curiosity and imagination." We hope to return for more of Mochi Wala's infamous tales.

“What Magical Tales of the Mochi Wala adventures await us in the next instalment? A teaser for now…”

The Greedy Rakshasa

Not too long ago, in the charming and old-fashioned village of Vadgaon Sheri, nestled between the mighty Brahmaputra River and the vast ocean, two childhood friends, Kanip the fisherman and Balu the cobbler, shared a bond that was as sturdy as the crafts they practised. Kanip spent his days on the river, casting nets into the shimmering waters.

At the same time, Balu worked diligently at his modest shop, repairing worn sandals and stitching leather with precision born from years of practice. Their friendship was forged in simplicity and trust, each relying on the other in their own way.

Whenever Kanip's nets were frayed, Balu's skilled hands would bring them back to life, weaving strength into every thread. In return, Kanip would ferry Balu across the Brahmaputra in his sturdy boat, helping his friend gather rare materials for his leatherwork. As the sun dipped below the horizon, the two would meet by the riverbank, sharing tales of their day. The scent of the sea mingled with the earthy aroma of the village, creating an atmosphere of camaraderie and contentment.

One fateful moonless night, Kanip was going home after a long day on the water. His woven basket brimmed with a fresh catch, their silvery scales gleaming faintly in the dim light. The air was thick and salty, carrying an unsettling stillness that seemed to weigh on him more than usual. He tried to shake off the unease, focusing on selling his fish at the market and earning enough to provide for his family.

As he entered the dense forest path, the shadows seemed to close around him. An eerie silence replaced the usual rustle of leaves and insects chirping. Suddenly, a sly, guttural laugh echoed through the trees. Kanip froze in his tracks, his heart pounding in his chest.

"Who's there?" he called out, his voice trembling.

The laughter grew louder and closer until it seemed to surround him. A Rakshasa emerged from behind a gnarled oak, its crimson eyes glowing like embers in the darkness. The creature's skeletal frame was draped in tattered rags, and its tangled hair moved as if caught in an invisible breeze. Kanip's knees threatened to buckle under the weight of his fear.

"A mortal with a basket full of fish," the Rakshasa sneered, its voice slithering like a serpent. "But your catch carries a scent far more tantalising than mere fish. Are you hiding something from me?"

Kanip stammered, his words barely audible. "I… I'm just a humble fisherman. These fish are all I have to provide for my family."

The Rakshasa tilted its head, its sharp teeth glinting in the faint moonlight. "A humble fisherman, you say? Then you shall prove your humility by cooking these fish and feeding me every night. Fail me, and I shall feast on you and your family instead."

The creature's laughter echoed through the forest as it vanished into the shadows, leaving Kanip paralysed with terror. He stumbled home, his mind racing with the horror of what had just transpired.

From that night on, Kanip's life was no longer his own. Each evening, he would cook his catch and deliver it to the Rakshasa, watching helplessly as the creature devoured it with grotesque relish. Its burps reverberated through the forest, a mocking reminder of Kanip's helplessness.

The fisherman's once-thriving trade collapsed. The fish he would have sold at the market now disappeared into the Rakshasa's insatiable maw, leaving his family on the brink of starvation. Kanip grew gaunt and weary, his spirit crushed by the weight of his predicament. His wife noticed his growing despair, but Kanip couldn't reveal the truth.

Finally, Kanip sought counsel from his lifelong friend, Balu the cobbler. The weary and burdened fisherman poured out his woes, recounting the Rakshasa's menacing demands and the toll it had taken on his livelihood and spirit. His voice cracked as he spoke of the daily terror that now defined his existence.

Balu listened intently, his weathered hands still as he absorbed the gravity of his friend's plight. "Ah," he said, his eyes narrowing with concern and determination. "No wonder I haven't seen you in days. This is your burden." He rubbed his chin thoughtfully, his brow furrowed. "Let us ponder a solution, my friend."

Balu was a man of practicality and creativity, and his small shop was a sanctuary for those in need. Leather scraps, tools, and unfinished sandals lay scattered around him, evidence of a life dedicated to his craft. Now, that craft would be tested in an entirely new way.

"I have an idea," Balu declared, his voice steady and sure. "I shall craft sandals—a masterpiece of leather and love. Perhaps this offering will appease the Rakshasa and convince it to release you from this wretched pact."

Kanip's eyes widened with a flicker of hope. "Do you think it will work?" he asked, desperation lacing his tone.

Balu nodded. "It's worth a try. If nothing else, we will show the creature that you are more than just a servant to its greed."

The following evening, Kanip trudged homeward, his basket of fish heavy on his shoulder. As he approached the forest's edge, the air seemed to thicken, and an unnatural chill ran down his spine. The Rakshasa materialised, its sinister laughter echoing through the trees.

"What have you brought me today, fisherman?" it taunted, crimson eyes gleaming.

Kanip's knees threatened to give way, but he steadied himself. "I have caught fish from the river," he stammered, "and I bear a gift for you."

"A gift?" The Rakshasa's curiosity was piqued. "What offering could a lowly fisherman have for a creature like me?"

With trembling hands, Kanip revealed the cobbler's creation—an exquisitely crafted pair of sandals. The Rakshasa reached out with its bony fingers, tracing the delicate stitching. For a moment, its cruel eyes softened.

"These are… beautiful," it admitted, almost grudgingly. But then its voice turned sharp again. "Do not think this absolves you. Serve my meal promptly or suffer the consequences."

Kanip's heart sank. Despite the gesture, his daily ordeal was far from over. The Rakshasa devoured the fish with grotesque relish, and Kanip returned home, his hope dimmed.

Despair gnawed at Kanip's soul. The next day, he returned to Balu's shop, his shoulders slumped and his voice heavy. "It didn't work," he admitted. "The sandals were not enough."

Balu frowned, his wrinkles deepening as he considered their next move. "Despair not," he said, his tone resolute. "We shall seek aid from *Varuni*, the ancient water spirit. She rules the river where you cast your nets. Surely, she will lend her wisdom and magic."

At dawn, the two friends knelt by the river's edge, their hands clasped in prayer. The gentle lapping of the water seemed to answer their plea, and soon, a shimmering figure emerged from the depths. Varuni, her liquid form glowing with otherworldly light, regarded them with compassion.

"Troubled souls," she murmured, her voice like a ripple. "What burden brings you to my realm?"

Kanip recounted his plight, his voice trembling as he spoke of the Rakshasa's greed and the despair that shadowed his days. Balu added his plea, his words filled with urgency and resolve.

Varuni's liquid eyes held both sorrow and determination. "Take this pearl," she said, conjuring a luminous droplet of her essence. "Offer it to the Rakshasa. Tell it that with this pearl, it will have abundance beyond measure—a feast eternal."

Clutching the pearl, Kanip and Balu retraced their steps through the moonlit forest, the path winding toward the Rakshasa's lair. The creature awaited them amidst twisted roots and shadowed foliage, its hunger palpable.

"What have you brought me now?" it growled, eyeing the cobbler suspiciously.

Kanip stepped forward, holding the pearl aloft. "This," he said, his voice steady despite his fear, "is a token of abundance. With it, you will feast eternally and need never hunger again."

The Rakshasa's crimson eyes flickered between the pearl and the two men. It reached out a clawed hand but hesitated. "This pearl is but a dewdrop," it sneered. "I crave oceans. Bring me a bag of pearls, and I shall leave you in peace."

Kanip's heart sank, and Balu clenched his fists. The creature's greed seemed insatiable, its demands ever escalating.

The Rakshasa's gaze turned to Balu. "And you, cobbler," it hissed.

"You have seen me. For that, I am bound by my nature to consume you."

Desperate and out of options, Kanip and Balu returned to the river, their steps heavy with dread. Once more, they called upon *Varuni,* who emerged with quiet determination.

"This creature's greed blinds it," she said. "Take this glass bottle. Tell the Rakshasa to enter the bottle if it desires a bag full of pearls. Once the bottle sinks to the riverbed, it may emerge to claim its prize—but never return."

With renewed hope, the two friends returned to the forest. The Rakshasa, its hunger and arrogance undiminished, awaited them.

Kanip repeated Varuni's message, his voice trembling but firm. The Rakshasa hesitated, its suspicion warring with its greed. Finally, it shrank itself and entered the bottle, its crimson eyes gleaming with anticipation.

Balu swiftly sealed the bottle, and Kanip cast it into the river. The water swallowed it whole, the current carrying it to the depths.

Varuni appeared once more, her presence a balm to their frayed nerves. "You are free," she declared. "The Rakshasa shall trouble you no more. It resides in the bottle, surrounded by fish—a captive audience for its insatiable hunger. Perhaps now, it will reflect upon its greed."

The two friends bowed deeply, their hearts lighter as they left the forest behind. The river whispered gratitude, and Varuni's wisdom echoed through their minds.

The Rakshasa remained trapped in its watery prison. Hours turned into days, and the creature's realisation grew: It had been outwitted. The water muffled its furious roars; greed was now its eternal torment.

"Oh, my greed," it lamented. "It has undone me."

In the village, Kanip and Balu sat by the riverbank, the morning sun warming their faces. The terror of the past days seemed a distant memory, replaced by a quiet sense of triumph.

"Thank you, Balu," Kanip said, his voice filled with gratitude. "You saved me—and my family."

Balu clapped him on the back, a broad grin on his face. "We did it together, my friend. And we'll face whatever comes next, together as always."

The tale of Kanip and Balu spread throughout Vadgaon Sheri, a reminder that even the darkest trials could be overcome with courage, friendship, and ingenuity. The river, the forest, and the village bore witness to their bravery, and their bond became legends.

Moral of the Story - Greed, unchecked, can ensnare even the most powerful. Once a fearsome creature, the Rakshasa fell victim to its insatiable hunger. True wealth lies not in hoarding but in balance, compassion, and contentment. And as Kanip and Balu proved, the strongest bonds are those forged in trust and love, unyielding even in the face of the greatest darkness.

9 789334 250930

Printed at Repro India Ltd.